AND...

THE

MIRROR

CRACKED

By

Monica Handy

This book is dedicated to every person trying to find their way in this life

Table of Contents

Table of Contents cont.

PART ONE

Have you ever just wanted to get away from yourself -
...Become someone else?

Me, Oh My- Look At My Better Life!

A thousand times a day she promised herself that she wouldn't look at the old photograph, but a thousand times, she lied. If truth be told, *looking*, had become her weird, little obsession, or maybe, even a ritual by which she held herself in comparison.

Studying the soft curves of the young woman's face, surmised that she could have easily been on the cover of any magazine. -Yet, the mystery of those faded scars loomed as large as the unintentional cleavage, shown beneath sagging garments. This photo was a ghostly depiction of someone who wanted to *beat the odds.* That was the lesson that she would take from the photo on this day; tomorrow, she would learn something else.

The light rap on the door shifted her attention. "Come in," she called from the desk.

The door opened just enough for her assistant to stick his head in.

"All the department heads are gathered in the main conference room, per your request, Ms. Burrows..."

"Thank you, Clive. I'll be joining everyone, momentarily."

Satisfied, he closed the door, leaving Deborah to prepare for the meeting that had the entire office buzzing. No one, not even her longtime confidant, Clive, knew what she was about to announce. Hell, he didn't even know that beneath the calm veneer and flawless makeup raced the heart of a girl who still chased dreams like they were butterflies. All he knew, was that she captured them. With that, she closed the drawer on an old photograph and began her walk down the champagne and glass corridor of *GRACE Enterprises.*

Entering the tense conference room, her eyes had barely settled on all the questioning faces when longtime partner, Curt Cavanaugh went for the juggler!

"Really, Deborah?" Tumbled his farm---boy accent! "...In the middle of the day? During Sweeps Week?! Has peace reigned in the Middle East? Has Texas sided with Obama on gun control?!"

Whenever the middle-aged, Texan, who was also head of *GRACE broadcasting*, took the reins, someone was going to give him some answers!

"Funny, you should mention Texas..." Deborah began, but was quickly interrupted by Chief Editor of *The GRACE News Paper*.

"I'm with Curt on this one!"

"Hmmmm... Well-uh," Deborah syllabized, if you're with Curt, then who's *"with"* me?"

"That's not what I meant," Phyllis Gordon said, apologetically.

"I know exactly *what both* of *you* meant! And now that we know how valuable your time is, perhaps you will *lend* me your attention."

The room grew silent, yet poised with an impatient energy!

"Thank you", she said calmly. "As you know, the rumor-mill has been grinding out tales of my alleged affairs with everyone from Tyler Perry and Jamie Foxx, all the way to a pubescent cabana boy, I said "hello" to, in Madrid. It is, to say the least, ludicrous!" The others stiffened in their seats, bracing for the impending news.

"...So, to put a stop to this, I will invite the press to a gala I am hosting at the *Le Chateau Martinique*- just outside of Chicago.

"I know the place," Clive piped in. "But isn't it seasonal and only reserved for dignitaries?"

"Way ta go, Clive!" Grumbles an already aggravated Curt! So now the boss lady isn't good enough to eat with the top dogs?!

...Without taking his gaze off Deborah, Clive tried desperately to retrieve his fumble!

"You know that I, above everyone, believe your position is above and beyond reproach...

"...But not beyond your brown-*nose*, you kiss up!"

Deborah cut Curt a paralyzing look in the midst of his display. He was merely fueling the other 'Clive-Haters', taking them further and further off base!

"...As I was saying", Clive continued, "The type that frequent that establishment hate the press, i.e., us!"

"Clive, *I am* the *type* that frequents that establishment, or will be when I announce my marriage plans to Senator Taylor..."

Suddenly, time stopped; the room took a deep breath and then exhaled mass hysteria!

"Down South, Senator Taylor," spat an enunciating Phyllis? He's an old, white, republican, for God's sake!"

"Senator, 'boil your balls in oil if you're gay, having premarital sex, or a single parent' – Taylor?!"

This last remark, made by Richard Hawthorn cast a palpable loathing for her husband-to-be that ruminated way past a fleeting moment. The thin but muscled, Brit was a fashion king who handled all Marketing, PR, and Social Media. It could be said that he painted the image for how *Grace Media* was perceived. However, at times, Richard suffered from the well discussed delusion of forgetting that he was an employee and not in charge. The delusion often displayed itself as verbal effrontery, because words were Richards's favorite thing, in the whole, entire world. Only, this time, her *life* was his target.

The insults that flowed so vehemently, were imposing straws on a preloaded, top heavy camel! There were also rumors that Senator Jentezen Taylor loathed blacks, which, should have, in Deborah's opinion, made them reconsider the man that they were judging so harshly.

Curt, who still couldn't believe his ears, leaned in on white knuckles, atop the conference table and spoke in slow, deliberate phrases... "Now darling', I know the ratings could be higher, but we don't need a half-assed stunt, as a boot strap. We'll be fine!"

Jumping to her feet! "How dare you! Ten years, helping you run this Enterprise... One would think I'd earned just a little more respect!"

Curt was swift on the rebound, "Might I remind you how *GRACE* Enterprises was born? Judging from that blank stare on your face, I think not!"

"Curt, you are out of control!"

Brazenly undeterred, he locked his gaze on Deborah.

"We are already considered as little more than a rag magazine filled with second class journalism!"- Turning his gaze upon the shocked onlookers- "Just look at the colorful array of amassed talent!" Came his scathing sarcasm.

Clive, who felt brave enough to oppose their terrorist, stood up and pointed a narrow finger at Curt. "You need to hold your proverbial horses, Mr.!"

"How lame was that?" Curt ranted! "Holding our "proverbial horses" is why every other cable network is beating the firestones off our rims!"

"Have you been drinking, old chap?" Came Richard Hawthorns, snide remark.

"Don't get me started on you, Richard! ...Pimping boys, right out of the college dorms!"

"How many times must I remind you? It was an *escort service,*" Richard said calmly, "...developed to help pay our tuition. Now that's E-nough, Curtis! How long must we endure this ranting?"

"For as long as these lungs can draw breathe, buddy boy!" Turning his gaze back on Deborah- "Seems to me," posing his hands as if displaying a marquee--- "you wanna add another attraction to this circus entitled:

"Rag Mag Supports Satan! News at ten!"

Deborah's eyes betrayed her poise, telling a story of shock and sadness. Her longtime partner and friend seemed to be having a nervous breakdown right before her eyes, and short of calling security, she was helpless to stop it.

After several moments, which felt like an eternity Deborah somehow found her voice and said, "Are you done? May we proceed?"

Looking, unflinchingly into the eyes, he loved so dearly, he began to lower his arms and nod his head. "Yes, Deborah... I am *so* done..." With that, he took a few steps back, turned and left.

The Bomb Dropped- Now Here Comes The Boom

The next morning, Curt made his way to the executive suites, checking every office until he found Clive in the men's room. "What cock-uh-mammy schemes do you and the boss-lady have going on?"

Eyeballing Curt's disheveled appearance, with great disdain-

"Not this morning," responded a reserved Clive. "...Not in the mood!"

"Oh-That's right... Just twitch your tight little ass on back to Deborah while the rest of us burn!"

"No one is burning, Curt. And the only thing twitching is your career! So I'd watch it, if I were you!" "Yeah, buddy boy, I'm watching alright and so should you! Don't you know when powerful people wed, it's not called "marriage, it's called a *"merger"?!* In the process we become assets! ...Usable and disposable "assets!"

Okay", Came Clive's high browed response. "I don't know what you've been smoking, but I gotta tell ya Dorothy, we "are" still in Kansas. People with different backgrounds still fall in love. Perhaps they will be good for one another- I don't know. But the point being made here, today is, know when to back off! … Leave well enough alone. You need to learn some decorum and your place!" He annunciated.

"My place?" Curt curtailed. "My 'place' is preserving what these two hands helped to build from scratch …So your sorry ass can float to work every morning!"

"Perhaps you'd like to take two steps back and bring it down a notch," Clive calmly told the man whose Converse-All Stars were flush against the tips of his Stacey Adams. "Besides, I think you're just jealous that you won't be Deborah's Go-To, guy, anymore. …And, I'll reiterate, *They could very well be good for one another.*"

"*Good for One another?*" Curt snarled! "Really?! An, '*I wanna save the world*', flower child, and a *ruthless barracuda,* locked in matrimony?! Am I the only one who can see this bomb about to blow?!"

Backing away from Curt, Clive moves to the sink to wash his hands and pat up his tapered waves. I really think you're underestimating Deborah- and like I said, quit smoking."

That being said, Clive exited the men's room, leaving a frustrated and disheveled Curt, alone.

*THE PAST

1983-Wake Up and Smell the Coffee! Nerds Need Lovin' Too

Melody woke up, partially roused by the smell of fresh brewed coffee and pork bacon sizzling in a frying pan. She clung to the warmth of the covers a few seconds longer before sitting upright and rubbing slumber from her brown, doll---like eyes. Out of nowhere a smile crept up from the memory of last night and found its way across her glowing face. As was her subconscious habit, Melody grabbed the heart-shaped locket that she never removed, twisting the chain around her finger.

"Five minutes!" Yelled up her portly Aunt Vicky. "Breakfast will be on the table! You hear me gurl?"

"Yes, Aunty. I hear you. How could I not?"

"What'd you say?"

"I said, good morning," practically floating down the stairs and to her seat. She was still daydreaming when her Uncle Bob left the breakfast table, with his green mug and sports section. Funny how even his eyebrows raised when she failed to say her usual, *"Love you, Uncle Bobby. "* She just bit into the crisp bacon and chewed mechanically.

"This is really good bacon, Aunty."

"Gurl," came Vicky's urban tone! You been eatin' that bacon ever since you were four years old! Heck, me and your momma used to eat that when we were girls! What's got you so ringy-dingy this mornin'?"

"Ringy Dingy?" Asked Melody.

"Well, when you came into the kitchen you didn't walk, honey; you floated!"

"Floated?" trying to laugh off what she knew was the truth. "Aunty, you are so funny."

"...And now you're complimenting somethin' that you been eatin' for years, baby?"

Melody watched the wise woman brush graying hair out of her face while piercing her with those *knowing* eyes.

"What's his name Melody?"

"Name?" Melody asked.

Vicky looked around the country style kitchen and then peeked beneath the table. Automatically, Melody began to look too. "Aunty, what are we looking for?"

"The echo, child! You're repeating every word I say. Now, I ask you for the boy's name!"

Melody began to laugh, "His name is Gary Williams and he is my love..."

Vicky stared at the seventeen year old girl who was gnawing fat from the bacon rind. "...Your love?

Well, does this love of yours have a job, go to school, pull out your chair, or open your door?"

"Aunty, this is not the seventeenth century! ...And, yes, he does have a job."

"What about school?"

"He graduated already!"

"So he's a *MAN*?!"

"We are only a few years apart! Calm down, Aunty!"

Shifting her tone from aggression to calm reasoning, "In some cases "a few years," might as well be a lifetime, especially if you're on a fast track to success and he..."

"He, what?" Quaked Melody. You have never met him and already you are forming opinions!"

"...This is not hard to do when you ponder what his reasons might be, for dating someone still in high school."

Dropping the favored rind in lieu of defending her prince charming, "See! That's the problem," Melody proclaimed with greasy lips and hand gestures! "He sees me differently... He treats me like a queen! He sets me up high, in a special place..."

Raising a graying brow, Vickie's calm demeanor broke! "Speaking of *"special places,"*-has he seen yours?"

With all the indignation she could muster, "Aunty, how could you ask me that?!"

Of all the slang terms that she struggled with, *Dime---Piece* wasn't one of them. To be a *"Dime"* meant you were fine as hell, and as such, deserved special treatment, i.e. getting picked up from school every day and eating Burger King Whoppers whenever you felt like it! ...And dog-gone-it; she felt like it!

"Ms. Melody Renee Baxter!" Came Reverend Rodgers baritone voice. "You are supposed to be tutoring Lee-Roy today!"

"Today, Reverend Rodgers?"

Looking behind him and causing the others to look too. "What you looking for Daddy?" Came Lee-Roy's effeminate voice.

"I could have sworn I heard an echo. Yes, *TODAY*, Melody! ...Well?" Noticing her apprehension, "What's it gone be, child?"

With that Melody looked at Gary who stared straight ahead. The Reverends son, Lee-Roy was no help either as he pulled his tattered binder closer to his chest.

With one finger he motioned Melody to his side and then kissed her full on the lips.

Between the lingering kiss, Reverend Rodgers' venomous stare, and Lee-Roy clearing his throat, *'awkward'* could not even begin to describe the way Melody was feeling. No one had ever stood up to Reverend Rodgers and no one had ever kissed her like that!

BUMPING ALONG

The old church van for Mount Olive Apostolic Church must have hit every bump in the road and at some point caused the two teens to hit their heads on the vans ceiling!

"Dad, please! We wanna get there in one piece!"

"Hush up, boy! Can't you see Sister Baxter is in deep *"deep"* trouble?"

"Trouble?" Melody repeated.

"Lord, there's that echo again! Yes, Melody, *"trouble"* with a capital "T"! That man you seeing, aint no good! I know the type! He will break your heart and ruin your future... Furthermore, your Aunt Vickie would have a fluxuating fit, if she knew the company you were keepin'! And let's not even talk about your Uncle Bob!"

"Please don't tell my Aunt Vickie!"

"Child, how can I 'not' *tell* your Aunt Vickie? Bless her soul; workin' six night shifts a week at the hospital to make ends meet! She and Bob have had the church praying for you since you've been in their care. That's twelve years now! Then God has gone and blessed you to get a scholarship to North Western University so you can be a doctor and come back to help your community!"

Inside her mind, Melody was screaming, "But I don't want to be a doctor! I want to breathe and have fun like everybody else!"

As though the reverend had heard her mental ranting's he turned to look her dead on and said, "Melody, you're not like everybody else."

The van parked on a block lined with brick bungalows, in a middle class, Chicago neighborhood. It was the month of April and the weather was warm enough to draw people out, onto their porches. As they exited the van, various neighbors greeted the austere pastor with pleasant tones. However, Melody noted that there was one voice amongst the crowd that wasn't so friendly.

"Wuz up, Luh-Roy?" Scoffed their schools, star quarterback, whose boyish muscles and football jersey spoke for themselves.

"It's *Lee* not "Luh!" Corrected the baritone challenged, Lee-Roy. His response was so hostile that it caused Melody to stop and turn around.

Once inside the house, they were herded by one of the church mothers into the walnut and red brocade dining room. Melody's eyes widened to take in the soul food feast, and then closed as the man of God said grace. What followed in a silent procession, were bowls filled with hot steaming neck bones and potatoes, rice with black eyed peas, and stuffed pork chops. Fried catfish, greens, okra, spaghetti and cornbread were lifted up as well. There was one small bowl of jambalaya that sat and remained just north of Reverend Rodgers left elbow-which no one dared to reach for.

Speed walking on little short legs that never seemed to tire, Mother Juna served iced tea to everyone and then, without warning, planted a big reddish-orange lip smudge on Melodies forehead!

"Good to see you baby! You came on the day we warmed up every left over in the fridge! Now eat up and I'll prepare Sister Vickie and Brother Robert a plate to go!"

"Yes Ma'am," she replied, while secretly fighting the urge to rub thick clots of lipstick from her cheeks and forehead

She remembered countless occasions of trying to escape the exuberant touchy-kissy,

Sister Juna, only to be bum rushed from a blind side!

The chocolate skinned, round woman who religiously wore every piece of jewelry she owned, was kind, and exuded a type of selflessness that demanded love. It showed in her humble service at church, in this home and the tireless care-taking of Reverend Rodgers. People often talked about her choice of style, but truth was, she loved colors, whatever the combination, they were her righteous and independent statement.

Her thoughts were interrupted by the lanky Lee-Roy's foot that kept kicking her, by-now, bruised shin. He kept motioning with his eyes and head to move into the other room.

As bad as she wanted some of that peach cobbler and lemon meringue pie she wanted him to stop kicking her, more!

"May we be excused, Daddy?"

"Son, you barely finished your food."

"I know, but there is so much work to do..."

The reverend looked, tilted his head and then waved them away.

Once inside the den area, Lee-Roy closed the wood paneled doors and turned on the stereo. He cut the volume down, real low and then began to dance with moves and rhythm that Melody found embarrassing and ridiculous! After ten shocking seconds she moved quickly across the room and shut the music off!

"Boy, cut that out! Your daddy aint gone kill me!"

"Oh please! My daddy will be eating for at least another fifteen minutes and then he'll be on that prayer line for an hour. Sister Juna gets right on that prayer line with him just to say, *"Amen"* in all the right places. Now what?" he asked arrogantly.

Melody watched helplessly as he cut the music back on and continued to thrust his pelvis!

"O.K. Have it your way, Michael Jackson!"

"Do you really think so?" he said, while grabbing his crotch and moon walking across the room."

"Uh-No! Now get your books so we can wrap this up."

Lee-Roy stopped dancing. "Do you really think that you're here to help me study?"

"Well, that's why your daddy came and found me…"

"My *"daddy"* has nothing to do with this! Before my mother went to that nut house, she taught calculus… So, baby doll, I eat, sleep, and drink formula conversions and derivatives. All I had to do was fail a few exams to get you here; or manipulate Pops to get you here!"

Melody found herself blinking as if specks of dirt had blown into her eyes. And then for one brief moment, she had to examine the phrase, *"baby doll."*… But the truth was, she really couldn't believe her eyes… Or was it her ears? This frail boy who wore pants that were just beneath the flood line had morphed into someone with personality and hints of sexual prowess. Still Melody perceived and discerned gender confusion.

"So what do you want from me?"

At the end of her question Lee-Roy's eyebrows arched and a strange look came over his face. He then proceeded into a full--fledged, and what can only be described as, a *"Michael Jackson"* spin. His sudden *stop* found him posed with one hand in the air and the other groping his scarce crotch. "I wanna be cool! I want some freedom! I want some of what you're having!"

Melody rolled her eyes and jumped to her feet! "I'm leaving, you jack ass! I didn't come here for this retarded stupidity!"

"To be frank with you, it's a little rude to use "retarded" and "stupidity" in the same sentence. And to be honest, I thought you might feel this way."

Inside Melodies mind were a dozen questions brimming to be released but nothing perplexed her more than the wickedness used to manipulate his father.

"… And that's only because…" his steady voice drawing her away from her own thoughts "you don't see the big picture. As a matter of fact, in the back of your mind you're probably wondering, what's in it for me?"

Tilting her head and folding her arms, "Yeah! What's in it for me?"

"Well as far as I can tell, you and your new boyfriend's time is limited to the hours you can explain away to Sister Vicky. And from the way y'all be cozyin' up after school and on your job, and during your volunteer hours at the library, I'd say you could use some more quality time..."

Oh-My-God! You've been spying on me?!"

"I needed you! I mean, *I needed to*!" But, whatever the case you know I'm not lying."

As much as she wanted to turn and leave, she knew Lee---Roy Rodgers had done his homework. She also knew that she was willing to do anything for more precious time with Gary--- and here lied her time clock; pretending to tutor this creep! "Alright, she sighed, "what do you want?"

*PRESENT DAY

Brick Bracks, Nick Nacks and Howdy Do-s

The view from Jentezen Taylor's penthouse was breath-taking! The sun was setting over Lake Michigan and the silhouette of Chicago's skyline rose and fell like shadowy metropolitan mountains.

Over her shoulder, Deborah could hear her husband, to-be, talking on the phone. ...Something about "Trojan Horses, Brotherhood" and "Not knowing What Hit Them". In between *guffaws* he gave orders by way of pointing, to his assistant, Dora Floors; a stiff board of a woman, who never smiled. She was almost always by the Senators side to the point of his next move already being a foregone conclusion... There was so much going on, with the following year being an election year, and their upcoming wedding. Plus, his family was learning to feign just the right expression as they adjusted their racial palates to this particular brand of bliss. ...After all, when Jentezen Taylor has his mind made up there is no persuading him otherwise!

Hanging up the phone and waving Dora into an adjoining room, his attention turned to Deborah.

"Come here darlin'! I haven't forgotten about you."

As she swept over, and into his arms, she had to remember to pace her steps, for fear of running into his embrace. She wondered if the way she so desperately loved him, showed. She wondered if he knew how safe he made her feel after a day of being devoured by the needs and wants of others...

"You could have fooled me," she said softly, enjoying the feel of his chest beneath the weight of her weary head.

"Awww- now!" Stepping back to look deep into her eyes. Let me make it up to you. Name any place, and we'll go, just like we used to! Just me and you- tonight!"

Deborah backed away, and turned around. "Oh Jentezen, I understand what a pressing time this is for you. I also understand that even if we went to Mars, some Martian would appear, handing you a cell phone."

Coming up from behind to comfort her, "I had no idea that you felt this way. I've been neglecting you, so. I'll have Dora hold all my calls for the rest of the evening."

As Deborah turned back into his embrace a sharp memory eclipsed the moment causing her to become statue-still....

"Debby!" came Jentezen's one attempt to jar her. "Are you alright?" Then, his cell phone rang and like a loyal servant, he answered, backing away from his bride--to-be.

DEBORAH'S BACKWARD SPIRAL

In the hushed dimness, twelve years disappeared as Deborah's mind continued its backward spiral, to the downtown, Chicago Metra Station. The chill of that rainy, October evening, clung to the vivid memory of rush hour commuters in a hurry to go home, but unable to go anywhere. Her own train was delayed for an hour due to the storm, but she was not disturbed in the least. All that she could think about was, "how badly she wanted the columnist position at the Chicago Sun." Granted, it was a small column on neighborhood news, and was in no way equal to Mary Mitchell material, but one day, it might be!

The very possibility of landing the job sent her stilettos clicking to a nearby pub that had great chili and friendly service. She was determined to have a "faith" celebration! Her spirits dampened a bit, upon seeing the place packed with overcoat wearing travelers who inched across floors padded with rain-soaked cardboard.

"I'm afraid it's gone be a minute." Said the young, waitress.

As Deborah shook her head and turned to walk out, a gentleman, seated just to the left was kind enough to offer her a seat. "I'll be leaving shortly, if you care to sit down?"

A prolonged---"Uhhh," gave Deborah just enough time to scan the room once more for available seating. Finding none, she resolved to take the offer and removed her coat. "Thank you for your kindness. Can I buy you some coffee?"

"The gentleman seated across from her never looked up from what turned out to be a tattered magazine.

"No, thanks," lifting his hand in a gesture of acknowledgment.

"Small chili and hot tea, please." She told the waitress.

The pot of tea arrived first, and as she prepared and sipped the welcomed heat, she couldn't help notice the dark curls that hung with unkempt disdain, on her good Samaritans forehead. She wanted to- No, *needed,* to see his face.

"Would you care for some tea?" She asked, while craning her neck beyond his make-shift wall?

Suddenly, the magazine came down and she found herself *caught* by the unexpected eye-to-eye contact!

The corners of his mouth turned slightly upward, into a quick smile. What turned out to be piercing, hazel eyes, were also tired eyes. He had a five o clock shadow that whispered of him being forty-plus years old. Yet, he was boyishly handsome in a way that stimulated her, deep down inside.

Smile intact- "No, thank you." The Samaritan drawled.

"Excuse me?"

"You asked if I wanted some tea. The answer is, "No, Thank you."

Deborah felt silly, but quickly recovered. "I take it that you're not a Midwesterner?"

"Now, what gave me away?"

They both smiled, and Deborah extended her hand... "Deborah Burrows"

Accepting the gesture, "Sounds like a Hollywood name. My names, Curt Cavanaugh"

"... And you sound like a news anchor."

"Well, good for you darlin'! Cause that's what I am."

"Get out of here!" Deborah said with an exuberance that surprised even her.

"Yup! In West Texas. I was also program manager for thirteen years..."

"You're a long way away from home. Are you covering a story here?"

"I'm just taking some accumulated vacation time, deciding if I ever want to go back."

This silenced Deborah, because she couldn't think of anything better than being in media. It was her own, personal dream... "Oh, I see."

"Don't look so sad, darlin'. It'll all pan out. What about you? What's your story?"

"It's not as interesting as yours, I'm afraid."

"You never know. Try me?"

"I'm waiting to hear from The Chicago Sun. I applied for a columnist position."

"Is that right?   So what is it you'll be writing about?   ...And please don't tell me rehashed regurgitation!"

"Excuse me?"

Don't be offended, darlin!"

"My name is Deborah.   And, to answer your question, Mr. Cavanaugh, I plan on taking a run-of-the-mill, news piece about community issues, and using it to give ordinary people a voice!"

"Is that so? And what will your editor be doing while you rearrange the universe?"

"Ha-Ha! Very funny! Of course you just don't sweep in and take over. You gradually turn things around. Besides the news today is so one dimensional! If given a chance, people can come up with their own solutions!"

Grabbing his coat and the tattered magazine, made Deborah a little sad. She had to admit, she loved feeling and hearing her own passion for the Media industry. It made her feel a certain validation. Besides, no one else ever believed in her dreams, nor supported them.

"I've got to go, dar... I mean, Deb-o-rah," being careful to enunciate the syllables of her name. "My train will be here in three minutes. It was nice to have met you. You've got enough heart to maybe change this old world of ours! Good luck to you!"

Again, their eyes met and locked into a drinking gaze...

"You're gonna go far- trust me."

With that, her not so tall but definitely handsome, Samaritan swept out of her life and she felt the familiar slump find its way into her back again as she dug into the lukewarm chili.

It was nearly eight thirty by the time she reached her warm, dry apartment. A hot bath and a warm bed beckoned her, so much so that she left a trail of clothing on her way to the bathroom. Within an hour, she was snug and drifting off to the sound of raindrops tapping on the window pane. "Get up, gurl! You wanna be late? You gotta get to work!" Came the familiar voice.

Then there was that infernal shaking of her left arm! "Wake up!"

Deborah sat straight up, looking around the dark room for signs of the old woman who insisted that she wake up! Only, there was no old woman, just Jentezen rousing her from sleep. "Wake up darlin'. Its late- You must have drifted off."

Sure enough, she had fallen asleep as she drifted backward into her past. Now here was her future husband, staring her in the face and all she wanted was to go back to sleep.

**THE PAST

Hey Man, I'm Not Your Boy Toy!

The evening brought with it a sudden chill, causing the already anxious, Lee-Roy to pace, back and forth, outside the library. He was waiting on Melody, but of course he had told Reverend Rodgers that they were on a study date. Truth, be told, they were going to the mall, alone, with no supervision, where he could be *"cool"* in public. In his mind, this "public" display of rehearsed savvy would get girls to like him! The thought was, at times, so overwhelming that he found himself giggling out loud!

One more peek through the glass doors revealed that Gary had emerged from amongst the shelves to romance an "off-the-clock" Melody. And from the look of things, she was in no hurry to get away.

...But Gary was imposing on his time, which was limited!

As he grabbed the door handle to go in, a familiar voice from behind stopped him in his tracks.

"What's up Luh---Roy?"

Before Lee-Roy even turned around, He knew it was Dennis Reeves, who lived across the street from his house.

"I told you, Dennis, Its "Lee" not "Luh!"

It surprised Lee-Roy that his stern correction and unshifting eye contact did not deter the muscled jock from entering his personal space.

"Look-uh-here," said Dennis', slipping an arm around Lee-Roy's shoulders and walking him toward a secluded, back entrance. "Now, you know, and I know what happened last year in David Henrys basement!"

The weight of those words caused Lee-Roy's knees to buckle, and his eye contact to diminish into a shifty sort of shame.

"I thought no one was supposed to ever speak of that again, Dennis! You broke your own rule!"

"Maybe so. But I want a little more of that action!"

Lee-Roy looked at Dennis, devoid of a certain comprehension... "How could you ask me to do those things?

Denise who had now developed a certain saunter, replied, "Your dad used his juice as a preacher to get my dad to let you into our celebration! I was on the stairs listening in while they were talking... Your dad ask my father to let you into our football party, saying, "Maybe he'll man-up a little, if he's around boys like Dennis".

Lee-Roy's expression left no doubt that he was stunned and embarrassed.

"Yeah, that's right," continued Dennis. And didn't nobody force ya ta drink dat much booze!"

"I - I felt so uncomfortable.... I knew I didn't belong there..."

"Uncomfortable or not", the arrogant Dennis continued, "...the real 'LUH'-Roy showed up! "He laughed.

Enraged, Lee-Roy lunged at Dennis who with one swift movement dodged the attack and had Lee-Roy in a choke-hold. He, then whispered the next words in his ear with a slow deliberation...

"You are our toy, Boy! We own you! We want our dicks sucked like that on the regular. Got it?!

Lee-Roy, who was turning blue, gripped and clawed at his assailants arm for him to release the pressure!

"Do you got it?!"

Lee-Roy managed a laryngitis-ed, "Yes," and only then was he thrown to the ground!

As Dennis walked away, he turned back for a moment, spouting,

"My place, seven-thirty, on Saturday. My parents have a banquet." With that he brushed past Melody and Gary who were exiting the library. Melody did a double take, remembering the boy from the other night, but chose not to speak. Now, she wondered why Gary was pointing to the ally and laughing.

"Aint that yo punk-ass, boy, getting up off the ground, over there? "Melody turned, and sure enough, it was Lee-Roy patting his tapered Jerry Curl in an attempt to recover what dignity and composure those too short pants, would allow.

"Lee-Roy, what happened? Is that boy bullying you?" Before he could respond, Gary piped in with gay satire, complete with a lisp and limp wrist

"...I don't know girl- I think whatever happened, he liked it!"

For the first time, ever, Melody turned on Gary "Shut up! Can't you see this is serious?!"

Then it happened... A side of Gary emerged that Melody had never seen before! He grabbed her hair with one hand and slapped her face with the other!

"You're special because I made you that way! Other than that, you're just a regular piece! A cunt like any other of these hoes walking-Got me?!"

He never even waited for an answer-just jumped into his Mustang and sped away...

In that instant Lee-Roy Rodgers and Melody Baxter were forged with a bond that would never be broken.

**PRESENT DAY

Cotton Pickin' Yankees

Curt found himself at the Metra station, where he'd met Deborah so many years ago. His little Ms. Sunshine, had turned to the dark side and he needed *this* reference point to reconstruct what had gone so terribly wrong.

Senator Jentezen Taylor hated Civil Rights, Gay Rights, Abortion, Obamas stand on healthcare- Yet, claimed to love Jesus! He was of a money, power, opportunistic origin that linked him to a legion of so-called brilliant minds; minds that *made* things go bump, in the night. Senator Taylor and his sweat shop owning, sex trade operating, rice fields vested, cronies, had darker secrets that included Middle Eastern Oil, and the wars thereof. Then there were industrial pyramid schemes, responsible for the crumbling of fundamental American structures. ...Structures that allowed common people simple pleasures, like eating, keeping their homes and taking hot baths. Jentezen's money and influence was long and strong enough to have eyes and ears across the globe. So, the question remained, what did he want with *his* Deborah? That is what his undeviating and deliberate mission would be... Then he

would crush the wheels and pulleys of this man's merry-go-round, permanently!

The Chic and The Shank of It

Deborah, followed by Clive, walked gingerly through the Chateau Martinique, admiring the acclaimed, dining rooms and hanging gardens. This place, with its vaulted ceilings, brass moldings, and glass exterior walls was a testament of beauty! The temperature remained a steady seventy--five degrees throughout the changing seasons, and some sort of exotic flower was always in bloom. This is where they catered to the whims of the wealthy and a mistake could never be made. Even what seemed casual in nuance, was in actuality, quite deliberate.

"And that will conclude our tour" said the friendly, but apprehensive administrator. "Shall I be in touch with your staff for payment arrangements?"

"That won't be necessary," Deborah said coolly. We are prepared to seal the arrangements now.

Without another word, Clive removed a check book from his briefcase and began writing the agreed upon, figure.

"There is just one thing," Deborah added. "Please make sure that Senator Taylor's back is away from any outside, facing glass. - Jentezen has a thing about being able to see everyone and everything, at *all* times."

The administrator's eyebrows arched and his lips parted but nothing came out.

"Are you alright" questioned Clive?

"I'm afraid you'll have to excuse me- Am I to understand that this engagement party is for Senator Jentezen Taylor, of The Texas Taylor's'?"

"Yes, that is correct" Deborah answered.

The man, then touched what appeared to be a small button on his lapel, and spoke into an undetectable microphone. "May I have all hands in The Paradise Room, at once, thank you?" Both Deborah and Clive knew, what seemed to be a request, was in reality, a command.

Single filed, head waiters, planners, designers, chefs and a doorman entered the room. The administrator waved their attention toward Deborah-

"This is the future Mrs. Jentezen Taylor."

Everyone's expression reflected the task at hand, except for one waitress, whose brows arched in surprise! She was immediately dismissed and later seen leaving the premises, in tears.

"Her name," he continued, "is Ms. Deborah Burrows of Grace Enterprises. In three weeks, she will be announcing her engagement to Senator Jentezen Taylor. We will no longer be using the Magnolia Room, instead we will be upgrading to the Gold and Diamond Rose Petal motif. I will expect Ms. Burrows to be briefed on everything available to her through this upgrade"

The man made eye contact with Deborah and said, "Of course there will be no additional charge," -then nodded in a gesture of servitude.

However, Deborah didn't know whether to say "thank you" or address the blatant insult in a ghetto fabulous capacity! She chose the former, and smiled as she and Clive took seats that had not previously been offered. She almost made it past the hump of indignation, when Clive leaned over and whispered, "Told you so."

***THE PAST

Pinky Swear

The two of them, disheveled and disillusioned, stepped off of the city bus and walked slowly up the block to Reverend Rodgers house. Lee-Roy stopped short of the front door and led Melody through a side entrance instead. One look at them would reveal that they had not been studying at the library. Melody's eyes were swollen from the slap and so many tears, while Lee-Roy had suffered abrasions and a ripped jacket. They managed to make it into the room where Lee-Roy had originally shared his plan. For a moment, they both sat quietly and then Melody burst into tears! Lee-Roy wanted to comfort her but the shame and torment over his manhood retarded his movement. He didn't feel worthy enough to comfort anyone. In lieu of touch, he spoke soft, gentle words that comforted her from a distance. He knew it was working because she began to dry her eyes and focus on him.

"What did he do to you Lee-Roy? I swear I won't tell! You and I are locked together now. We are a team... Pinky swear," she smiled.

"Melody, I can barely stand the truth, myself."

With every good intention, Melody went over to console her new-found confidant, who side stepped her touch and tightened his already, folded arms. He kept his distance, almost as if he didn't want her to even look at him.

"Ok, now you're scaring me, Lee-Roy. What happened?"

Lee-Roy's knees folded as he slid down the wall, to the floor in a far corner and began telling the horrors he tried to forget.

"Oh my God," she whispered through fresh tears! "The football team?"

Tears began to flow down Lee-Roy's face-"I mean, I knew that I was different... I guess everybody can see that. But what they did was so brutal," he sobbed! And now they want more. ...Wish I could just change my name and move away where nobody knows me!"

"What are you talking about," Melody insisted?

"Dennis, is making sure that I come to another," -posing his fingers in quote, unquote signification- "gathering, on Saturday night..."

"And, if you don't?"

"He'll probably beat the crap out of me again! Enough about me. What are you gonna do with Sir Lancelot and his Mustang chariot?!"

"Ha, ha- very funny! He never heard me talk to him like that before" she half explained, half pleaded. "It caught him off guard..."

Lee-Roy wasn't buying it! "You sound just like Mrs. Rodriguez."

"Who, pray tell, is Mrs. Rodriguez, Lee-Roy?"

She's that lady who always waves a lace hanky when The Holy Ghost hits her!

Melody nodded in remembrance. "She used to come over, at least twice a week; crying every time. My daddy would take her into his study and Sister Juna would bring a box of tissues and two glasses of lemonade. Then the door would be closed for a half hour before they'd come out again."

"Reverend Rodgers was creepin' with the Mexican, church lady?!"

"That's what I thought... Until I put my ear to the cracked door. She was crying about how her husband hit her for nothin'! She said she would have dinner ready, the house clean and he would just lose his temper and start hitting her, for nothing!. She didn't know what to do…"

"Oh Lee-Roy! Stop right there. Once I apologize, Gary will too, and everything will be back to normal."

"Yeah, ok."

"It will! You'll see. And by the way, you can tell Dennis, "No!"

"And you can tell that drug pushin, woman beater, "No!"

Turning away from Lee-Roy and throwing her hands up-"I'm not doing this with you! I gotta go!"

Walking toward the door, she turned around- "By the way, Lee-Roy Rodgers, if you ever changed your name what would it be?"

Lee-Roy smiled, as though he had already given this plenty of thought. My name would be "Clive… Clive Hammond. I would be rich and perfect!

…And you, Melody, what would your name be?"

She tilted her head to one side and said, "Something strong... Something biblical... I got it! My name would be, Deborah- just like the prophetess in the bible. ...Deborah Burrows- because I'm gone plow my way through this messed up world!"

They both laughed a little and Melody went home.

PRESENT DAY

Every Garden Aint Eden!

Curt sat alone in the outer garden of the Chateau Martinique, staring at the engagement party within. This scene caused him such great unrest that not even the two billion dollar, a bottle champagne, could numb it. He watched Deborah's frozen smile circulate the room while Senator Taylor made huge arm gestures that suggested political promises to suckers with a vision! It was all one great big montage of schemes and bribes hosted by a love starved, flower child with fairytale dreams...

She had always been a go-getter! He knew it the first day he'd offered her a seat, in the crowded café. She was vibrant, fresh out of some night school, journalism class, and wanting to set the world on fire! At that point she didn't realize that he would be her kindling. He still remembered the look on her face when he gave her an abrupt "good bye", thinking she would never see him again. But unbeknownst to her, she had caused him to make a decision in just under fifteen minutes that he'd labored with for six months. He would take the position at the Chicago Sun as lead news editor, and hire Deborah, on the spot! After all, it had been sixteen years, and he was suffocating at WTEX. There seemed to be no fresh winds blowing. All the big news stories were manipulated to the point of being mere fabrication. Even as he sat here, big money was changing hands to keep foreign sex trade operations, undercover. To complicate matters, Liberals, who were vocally persuasive with the public, seemed to be dropping like flies, of the same respiratory infection that wasn't effecting anyone around them... Go figure? At any rate, he wanted O.U.T.-OUT!

The same day he made the decision to take the job was the same day he was shown a corner office, overlooking the Chicago River. The following day found him digging through boxes, scattered around that *state of the art*, office suite.

"Mr. Cavanaugh," came the throaty tone of his executive assistant, "would you like me to have someone gather all that paper and transfer the data to our system?"

"No, no, darlin'," tumbled his farm boy accent. "I've got my own system," spinning around to place the chipped, cowboy boot figurine on the mahogany desk.

With that, the six foot, African American blonde batted thickly coated lashes in silent disdain and asked, "Will that be all, Mr. Cavanaugh?"

Without even looking up, "Yes, Bernadine, that will be all. By the way... Can I call you Bernie?"

The administrator battered her lashes, shifted her weight to one side and was about to give insubordination a new meaning, when Deborah Burrows appeared in the open doorway.

"Is this the Editors office?"

"Yes it is. I was away from my desk. How may I help you?"

Before she could answer, Curt made eye contact with Deborah and spoke across Bernadine's shoulder. "Just come this way, *darlin'*. I mean, Deb--*o*--*rah*... Did I get it right?" came the southern drawl that wasn't quite so charming anymore.

Within a matter of seconds, Deborah's face shown a kaleidoscope of expressions, ranging from joy to confusion, then slight irritation, and finally resolve. Was this really happening, she thought?

As if reading her mind, Curt Cavanaugh half walked, half ran across the huge office suite, with an extended hand.

"Mr. Cavanaugh?" she asked, as her shoulder shook violently from the spirited handshake?

"Yes, Deb-o-rah, "ever mindful to annunciate, while leading her to a chair. "I do believe, you stated that you wanted to set the world on fire?"

Her eyes widened in response, not knowing if she should be flattered that he actually listened to her, or if she should be searching for malicious undertones...

"If memory serves correct," he continued, "you have this need to exercise an innovative brand of journalism that will cause the world to take an introspective view of itself, and just like that" snapping his fingers- "change will occur! Am I right?"

Deborah, jumped up with a force that ripped holes in the back of her panty hose! "How dare you set this whole thing up - just to make fun of me? I am twenty-five years old! A grown woman who has responsibilities! I don't have time for games!"

For the first time in years, Curt Cavanaugh was experiencing strange emotional sensations…. If she had known him better, she could have discerned that his delayed response translated as 'awe'. No one, ever yelled at Curt Cavanaugh!

"Ms. Burrows, please believe me when I say, that no one has rearranged the earth's rotation just to accommodate you. One thing you will learn about me," squinting as though the sun was in his eyes" I do not play games. I'm a hard and heavy hitter! If there's meat in a story, I wanna smell and taste it! Now, yesterday, in that café, you said you wanted to do something and it got my attention… Do you want it, or not?"

Deborah's prior stance melted underneath the weight of her dreams coming true. "Yes, Mr. Cavanaugh, I want it!"

"Bernie," He called, to no avail. "I mean, Bern-uh-dean!"

With the correct name, his administrator promptly appeared. "Could you get me all the video accrued by our news station on violent, neighborhood crimes- taking place in the last four months? I also want the names and contact info of the family, friends and witnesses who were interviewed about the crimes."

"Right away, Mr. Cavanaugh"

Turning his attention back to Deborah--- "You're in the big time now. Unfortunately, people are scared out of their wits because gun violence is running ramped in Chicago! People don't wanna come outside, nor send their kids to school! I want you to tap into the pulse of that fear and helplessness and dig until you find hope! Then let that hope guide your story!"

Deborah knew that she had been cast into the deep, but the look in this man's eyes was her anchor.

"You got me?"

"Got you!" She concurred.

"Good! Bernie will schedule your interviews and I expect results by Monday morning."

"Today is Thursday!"

"Then why are you still standing here?"

On that note, Deborah ran to go find Bernadine- She ran to feel the breeze of her dreams... But mostly she ran so that her past wouldn't catch her.

THE BRIBE TO BE

The engagement party was a smash hit! Even Jentezen's parents smiled convincingly when a toast was raised to the bride-to-be. Perhaps they were numb to the scandalous antics of Patrick, Jentezen's younger brother and decided to make merriment of the moment.

Clive, never more than ten feet away from his beloved, Deborah, was marvelous at hiding undercurrents of cynicism mingled with brotherly concern. But, she could tell, and had never seen him look so helpless.

Mostly everyone else seemed animated by the familiar spirits of champagne. There was high pitched laughter, and business men allowed the timbre of their tones to relax a bit. She, too had partaken, but the effects were lost on her, and she couldn't figure out why.

"Almost over," she thought, turning to look out at the manicured grounds. ...But what she saw startled her. −Standing, ever so still, was Curt staring back at her. He looked as though she had betrayed him somehow... "How dare he!" Her thoughts shouted... How dare he come here and make her feel bad about being secure! Yet she strained to detect some secret gesture that signaled, "Carry on." But there was none... Not even a wink or a smile... Just a cold knowing that never rested in peace.

PART TWO

The Bough Broke
(The Past)

COMIN' OUT OF CLOSETS AND RUNNIN' AFTER FOOLS

Lee-Roy rang the doorbell, convinced that the two self--defense moves he'd learned in gym class could at least keep a few of them at bay! His dad had gone to drive Sister Juna home, and was oh, so happy when he learned that his son had been invited to Dennis Reeves, football meeting.

The door cracked open just enough, for Lee-Roy to see the soft glow from the table lamp and no further. He waited for an invitation to come in and then realized that an eyeball was peering around the door at him. "Who's out there with you, man?"

"Nobody!" said Lee-Roy, trying to add some base to his voice. "I'm alone!"

"Better be! Get in here," Dennis demanded!

Pushing the door open, Lee-Roy stepped inside, peering around the dim room for signs of movement. Behind him, the door quietly closed and the locked clicked in place.

"Now, look Dennis," he began---"I know what happened last time, and you might wanna beat my butt every time you see me, but I just can't do it again! I'm not gonna be you all's sex slave!" There was no response, leaving him to pause in the silence... Something wasn't right... Turning around, he had every intention of asking, where everyone was- only, the frail, seventeen year old boy wasn't prepared for what Dennis had in mind. The handsome, young quarterback was dressed in heels, a mini skirt, and brassier. If that weren't cause for alarm, the purple lipstick was a blurring siren!

"Oh my God, Dennis- what are you wearing?!" The words seeped from his lips like a tire with a slow leak, edging Dennis from perversion to psychotic...

The bra-bound boy responded by lifting a seven inch blade to trace the circumference of his stained lips...

"What?" Came the eerie feminized tone. "Don't you like it?"

Lee-Roy was speechless as he watched Dennis' face contort with what his father called, "demonic disturbances".

"You're the faggot-bitch!" He yelled. I did this to make it easy for you! You thought you were gonna bang me?! Naw," he said, shaking his head slowly. "I'm rodding you OUT," he yelled!

Lee-Roy couldn't comprehend Dennis' need to be dominant versus his choice of attire. The contradiction was beyond rationalization, and he thought it best to slowly back away. He felt, that if he could put enough space between them, he may be able to turn and make a run for it! It was the small ottoman that undid his getaway, for the tumble he took found him looking up from the matching chair and into the eyes of a psychopath!

Dennis began to laugh and twirl around in the pastel mini skirt.

"Look man," came Lee-Roy's quacking effort at reasoning-"...It seems like you had a little too much to drink...."

"Shut up-Faggot and enjoy this show!" With that, Dennis spread his legs apart and did a quick drop-squat, while flexing his hips back and forth. One couldn't help but think, if there had of been a pole and the crowd was right...

Lee-Roy struggled to sit up-right in the chair, but Dennis took it as a sign of approval to move in closer.

Right up close and personal, Dennis flicked the mini skirt up for Lee-Roy to see what should have remained hidden. Closer and closer he came to his face until there was no doubt about what he wanted. He placed one hand on the back of Lee-Roy's head and allowed his knife-hand to relax. It was then that Leroy grabbed the knife and plunged it into Dennis' thigh! The sound the boy made was like some wounded beast! As soon as his eyes moved in shocked horror to the protruding knife, Lee-Roy used both feet to kick him down and run for the door!

His heart was pounding so loud he could hear it in his ears, and his lungs burned for oxygen! As he closed and locked the front door of his home, he heard his father's voice...

"How was the football meeting, son?"

When he turned around to meet his father's fading smile he began to sob...

I GOT MY MIND MADE UP

The sound in Vicky's voice was a mixture of pleading and mother-wisdom. "Don't go, Melody! You are ruining your future! That boy don't really care about you!"

For the first time, that morning, Melody stopped her mad scurry of gathering belongings to confront her aunt Vicky.

"Keep your voice down! The windows are up and he may hear you!"

"With all that loud music blaring, at seven o clock in the morning! He has no respect for this house or YOU! I don't understand! First Reverend Rodgers boy goes off and stabs Dennis Reeves, the star quarterback- which ended any future he had in football, and now you runnin' off with cat-trash!"

Melody rolled her eyes and grabbed her bags. "You're right, Aunt Vicky. You don't understand."

"Melody, I've seen his kind before baby...He only cares about himself..."

Down the stairs she went, refusing to be hindered.

"What about your life? The scholarships? Your mother?"

The last question stopped Melody in her tracks. "You leave my mother out of this! ...Always using her as a weapon to keep me in check!"

"Oh yeah?! Well the reason she aint here is because of a nigger like him!" Tears welled up in Melody's eyes. "You will say anything to keep me a prisoner! I thought you loved my mother! "

"I do", Vicky sobbed. "A part of me died with her."

"Well I'm not dying in her memories! I graduated and now I'm eighteen and there's nothing you can do to stop me!"

Vicky shouted as she opened the door, "Wait!" From her bosom came an old, laminated photograph. "I want you to have this..."

Melody looked briefly at the picture before shoving it into her purse. "So who is that haggard, dried up thing?"

"That was your mother, at thirty eight years old, just before your father beat her to death!" Melody lifted the silver locket from her chest and with a steady voice and unwavering eyes said, "This is the way I choose to remember my mother. " And then, she left.

FALSE TESTIMONY

When the ambulance arrived, Dennis was dressed in shorts and a football jersey. His leg, which still bled profusely was wrapped in a towel.

Neighbors lined each side of the street as their "neighborhood" hero was hoisted into the ambulance.

In court, the story went: *that even though Dennis tried to explain that the football meeting had been cancelled, Lee-Roy insisted on coming in, anyway. ...Said it would make his dad happy to know that he was hanging out with the fellas. Then he began acting weird and asked for a glass of water. "When I came back, he was wearing that,"* pointing to the bag labeled, *"evidence" which contained the skirt and bra... I tried to make him leave, but he used a knife to force himself on me! When I fought him off, he stabbed me!"*

Dennis' convincing state of hysteria won the Jury's "guilty" verdict, but worst of all, caused his father to hang his head and only acknowledge him in passing. That was worse than being sentenced to four years for aggravated assault and being placed in a psychiatric ward.

Two things that gave him a mild sense of victory, is that the knife had torn through muscle and chipped bone. The other, was that the state nut house was full, and he was being shipped to some comfy group home in Aurora.

FALSE PROMISES

"Where you gone go," he screamed?! ...Your Aunt Vicky and fuddy, duddy Uncle Bob don't want your sorry ass! And the deadline passed on them scholarships a long time ago!"

Melody sat there- Her eyes exploring the North Shore apartment, numb, to his reign of terror. She allowed her mind to escape by remembering the first day she'd seen the place. Gary excitedly, gave her the grand tour of their new apartment! She was mesmerized by the view of Lake Michigan, and the fancy faucets, in all three bathrooms. As if that weren't luxurious enough, her feet became lost in the plush, wall to wall, white carpet- and because of this, she believed he loved her.

It had been two years since Lee-Roy's conviction, and her messy departure from her own family. And, true to Aunt Vicky's prediction, she had made the worst mistake of her life. Her only solace became visiting Lee-Roy, every other weekend. The train ride was long, but peaceful, and sometimes, she even found herself making notes of what was happening around her. This allowed her to construct stories that entertained her incarcerated friend.

The facility wasn't bad at all. Lee-Roy wore regular street clothes, shared a room with some rich guy and was acing his accredited courses. From where she stood, all seemed normal, with the exception of the ankle bracelet and having to see a shrink twice a week... Her mind did, however, linger on all the new trinkets and gadgets he was sporting, like the Bulgari watch and the Hugo Boss belt. He said his roommate gave it to him because he was tired of his parents trying to buy his love with expensive gifts. And just like that, her concerns fell away. Besides, who was she to judge? ...For months, her every, teenage wish had been Gary's command. He was her knight in shining armor until his departures from their love nest were becoming earlier and his arrivals, later and her questions, more frequent until one day, he exploded with the same rage she'd seen in the ally with Lee-Roy.

Now, two years late, she was losing weight so rapidly that the clerks at the high end boutiques began to take notice. Her excuse was, wanting to fit into the perfect size two again. Gary had all but stopped coming home and his women called their home shamelessly, in search of their prince. Sometimes she would wake up to a stack of hundreds on the bedside table with a note that read, "Buy some food and pay the gas bill." Sure, she took care of those things and also registered into an evening journalism class for the fall session. The rest of the money, she began to stash in a safety deposit box, under an assumed name.

Oh yeah, Gary had thought of everything... Fake identification, passports, social security numbers; the whole gambit! She may have walked into this thing as Melody Renee Baxter, but she was exiting, Deborah Burrows.

THE ELUSIVE COOL

Billy Westinghouse, of the Illinois, Westinghouse's, was Lee-Roy's wealthy, rebellious, cell mate, and he was one of the blackest, white boys he'd ever met. Billy was always down for *"the cause,"* and whatever *"the cause"* entailed... Bombing abortion clinics, raiding and defacing pelt and tanning facilities, showing up at the "Million Man March" and lastly, giving all of his parents' choice Christmas pheasants to the underprivileged. Maybe it wouldn't have been so bad if five master chefs hadn't prepared them for the Westinghouse, annual Christmas Gala... But indeed they had. The way he tells it, the food line streaming from the South Side, Baptist Church stretched around the corner. And everyone went home with some pheasant!

Billy carried life around on his shoulder like it was a block that he dared family and random strangers to knock off. On the contrary, Lee-Roy was taught to revere the authority figures in his life, but somewhere along the lines, respect became synonymous with fear and it showed in his bowed head and hunched shoulders.

The two young men seemed to be complete opposites which presented an uncanny connection. ...Or perhaps it was a balance "of sorts". Whatever the nature of their connection, Leroy perceived Billy as having "the" missing factor that he so desperately longed for, and that was the *"elusive cool".* The five foot, nine inch, sun tanned, Billy was in possession of the *"elusive cool",* and didn't even seem to notice. He used it liberally in his saunter and piercing eye contact. He used it as though there were an unlimited supply and he had the monopoly. All Lee-Roy wanted was his fair share, therefore, he began studying his roommate's gestures, walk, and facial expressions. Then, when no one was around, he'd practice the "elusive cool" in the bathroom mirror by compressing his lanky, awkwardness into the persona of Billy's confident stride. There was no way this was going to come off as authentic... Not even to a blind man, and he knew it. Never-the-less, he continued the unintentional parody way longer than he should have. Even past the door opening and Billy, silently watching his buffoonery!

"Are you having some kind of break down?" Billy asked. "...And I thought you were a religious freak... Isn't your dad a Bishop, or something?"

In utter humiliation, Lee-Roy froze in the position that he believed paid homage to Billy's poise. He felt as if he moved he would shatter like bits of glass exploding from a window pain.

Billy turned from the bathroom and swaggered toward his bed. Lee-Roy's anal retention relaxed just enough for him to peer around the corner at the undisturbed Billy, who removed his sweat stained tee shirt and was now fishing through the trunk at the foot of his bed.

Lee-Roy, not quite over his shame, had to now, be creative with his voyeurism.

"Get out here, "Billy chuckled! "I know you're peepin' on me."

With that, Lee-Roy appeared from around his sacred corner just in time to smell the foul stench of Billy's joint.

"What are you doing?! Don't you know we can get more time for that?!"

Billy never paused, just drew deep and long from the marijuana cigarette.

"Sit down, Lee-Roy" he calmly demanded.

What Billy didn't realize is that Lee-Roy would very much like to sit down, only his feet wouldn't move and Billy's red-faced, eye contact wasn't making it any easier.

"Don't you realize that every guard in this place is on my daddy's payroll? Hell, I could go home tonight and come back in the morning if I wanted to. Now, come sit down."

Lee-Roy found his way over and sat on the very edge of Billy's bed. It was clear that he was out of his element, not knowing what to say or where to rest his roaming eyes. This became painfully evident when Billy passed him the joint and he flinched away causing his roommate to rare back in wild laughter. Then he suddenly stopped laughing and turned his piercing gaze on Lee-Roy. "My parents have a dossier on you about three inches thick! There is no way they would let me stay in the same space with you, not knowing who you are, or what you're capable of."

Lee-Roy said nothing, just continued staring at his shoes.

"So, you like boys? ...There are worse things."

Lee-Roy turned his head sharply and looked at his roommate through squinted eyes! "You don't know anything about me!"

"I know you aren't a killer!" He retorted. "And you never tried to wrangle my rump... Although, I can't explain what on earth you were doing in that bathroom when I walked in... Damn funny, though," he laughed. "My granddaddy always told me, *"Don't you ever let anybody know that you are afraid! I don't care if piss is running down your legs, you ignore it and stand up for what you believe in! "*

That's lesson number one, Lee-Roy Rodgers. Before you leave here, ole Billy gone teach you a whole lot more. Bout time you got a spine, Preacher Boy!"

PRESENT DAY

How Do Homes Become Hollowed Shells?

Reverend Rodgers stood in the doorway, looking at Lee--Roy through sunken, watery eyes. He never even attempted to smile. It was unsettling to see the definition of his father's age so deeply etched in his unflinching features.

"Aren't you going to let me in pops?"

"Pops?" Taken aback by the reference. "Where've you been", he responded? You've been out of that facility for six months. I received no phone call, no correspondence, nothing! And you just show up at my doorstep?"

Lee-Roy evaded the questions all together by side---stepping his father into the mahogany entryway. As his eyes drank in the familiarity of his home, he began to feel an embrace similar to that of a well-worn shoe. But something was missing... There was a lack of substance in the place he used to call "home". Suddenly it occurred to him that there was no aromatic smells coming from the kitchen, no church songs being belted out in a billy--goat timbre, no shuffling of house shoes across the aged wooden floors. And no lipstick smudged greetings from orange, stained lips!

"Where is she, Daddy?!"

"Where is who?"

"Mother Juna! Where is she?"

Slowly, he walked to the den, taking a seat and crossing his legs. Gripping the arms of his chair was a sign that he was ready to be forthcoming. "She's gone. ...Ran off with some fella who joined the church two years ago."

"And you let her?" Lee-Roy responded with pained amazement!

"I'm no jailer! I oversee a church. People have the right to come and go as they please!"

Lee-Roy felt overwhelmed, like he might explode! Usually his father was given the last word on any given subject- like it was some sacrificial peace offering. But as of this moment, he realized that he'd become a different Lee-Roy while locked away, and he just didn't feel like sacrificing anymore!

"Daddy, that woman loved you! She was faithful to you in her service. She wanted to do more than cook and clean for you!"

Uncrossing his legs signified that Lee-Roy had just crossed the line! "How dare you come in my house and question me about my decisions! That woman was a harlot! All that jewelry and makeup was a sin before Christ! She's lucky I let her work here for so long- Who else would have had her with all those psychedelic clothes? She looked like a hippy!"

"Daddy, you were lucky to have *"her"*! Now this house is an empty shell."

"Boy, don't you raise your voice to me! And I'll tell you another thing- this house belonged to your mother! No one else will ever fill her shoes! NO-ONE!"

Lee-Roy dropped his head wondering how one who led and fed so many didn't even know that he was starving for love and affection. He decided to abandon the subject for another one, hoping to make peace.

"So how are plans coming for Easter service? I can imagine the choir raising the roof off the building..."

"Lee-Roy," he said through a pained expression, "a lot has changed since you've been gone. When you first went away, support poured in from the community and other churches, out of respect for my plight- Not loyalty, but "respect". But after folks found out that Dennis Reeves was never gonna recover and go on to be a star quarterback, people began to leave. Oh, of course they did it with smiles and excuses, but, just the same, they left. A few stayed on, like Sister Vicky and Brother Bob, but the church is just as empty as this house." And then with words as sharp as the knife he'd stabbed Dennis with, his father said, "I'm just glad that your mother wasn't around to suffer such indignities."

"What indignities, Daddy?"

"So you want me to spell it out?!" Came the rhetorical question. "Ok, I will! The indignity of your persuasion!"

"I never said I was gay, you did! I stabbed Dennis in self-defense because *HE* was trying to rape me!" Tears began streaming down his cheeks when his father broke eye--contact and turned away.

"All the evidence points toward you!" Thundered his father's pulpit voice. I swear, you and that Melody Baxter must have been cut from the same cloth! The two of you were raised in the church, for God sake!"

Interrupting his father's tirade- "So, you never believed me?"

Reverend Rodgers, turned to him with tears in his eyes, "I had always hoped you'd turn out different... Be like the other boys... But you were soft and gentile, like your mother. No matter, how I told her to stop babying you, she wouldn't listen- just kept right on..."

"My mother loved me and nurtured my strengths! You, on the other hand, suck the life out of every living thing around you, using Jesus as a vacuum! Well, Reverend Rodgers," holding up his arms to display the surroundings, "welcome to your tomb!"

With that, Lee-Roy strode to the front door and didn't even look back as he said, "Good bye, Daddy."

GETTING PAST THE APPEARANCE

The look on Sister Vicky's face was a bizarre mix of shock and confusion. Before her, stood a taller and more confident Lee-Roy Rodgers, who assumed that it was alright to enter her home. What he didn't know was that she struggled internally with allowing the young felon past the threshold. On top of that, Bob had taken ill and was confined to his bed, upstairs. If something were to happen he couldn't be of much help to her.

"Lee-Roy Rodgers!" she said, feigning warmth and throwing her arms around his neck. Does your daddy know you're home?"

"Yes, Sister Vicky, he knows. I was hoping we could talk"

Vicky hesitated and then found herself thinking, *if he kills me Lord, then it must be my time to go!* "Come on in here, boy and sit down at the table. I'll warm us up some of these greens and neck bones."

Lee-Roy was grateful and finally felt the familiar spirit of *home.* All through the meal, they talked and laughed about heart-felt memories, both feeling the pressure of some things needing to be said.

"How is Melody," he ventured?

Vicky put her coffee cup back on the saucer. "No one knows, Lee-Roy. She ran off with that Gary character, not long after your trial. Lord knows we tried to stop her, but she was determined. We just pray her strength and ask God, daily to bring her back to us alive and well."

Lee-Roy was quite surprised to learn that he'd seen her since she'd left home but her beloved aunt and uncle had not. He chose not to share the news of her frequent visits to the facility.

"Now, it's my turn, Lee-Roy Rodgers. How is your daddy; up there in that big house, all alone?"

"Still, Daddy... He aint gone change. Sister Vicky, what happened to Mother Juna?"

Sitting back in her chair and taking a deep breath... "Well, Lee-Roy, when you left, it was hard on your daddy. He really wasn't the same man. It seemed his convictions about certain thangs took a heavy blow. Juna tried to comfort him, and if anyone said a word against you, she would cut 'em down like a lawn mower! She loved you like her own son." But your dad seemed to have his own ideas about what happened and how things could have been and she just couldn't bear the man he'd become. Gradually, she stopped going to the house and seems as soon as we got that new organist at the church, she took up with him and they got married." Vicky shook her head at the thought. "We all used to joke and say, "He must be color blind", because Juna loved her some colors!

Lee-Roy smiled. "Where is she now?"

"Out there in Schaumburg. The man was a chauffeur for some rich Jewish woman, and when she died, she left him everything! Aint that something? All those years of serving your father and now someone is serving her. Aint life funny?"

"Sure is," replied Lee-Roy. "It sure is" Well, it's getting late Sister Vicky. I better be heading out."

Vicky had been enjoying his company and was a little sad to see him go. "Well, ok. You tell Reverend Rodgers I said, hi."

Hugging her like a son hugs his mother, he promised to do so and left. Vicky turned on the news to keep her company while she cleaned up the kitchen, but had to sit down when she saw the picture on the screen and heard the lead story.

Gary Williams, a renowned drug runner for the Korean Mafia was found washed up on Chicago's lake shore in the Chatham area, early this evening. We will have further details as they surface during the course of this investigation...

She sat very still as if the earth would chip away beneath her feet. Her heart sank, wondering if she would soon be hearing news of her beloved Melody. And then there was Lee-Roy Rodgers, showing up on her doorstep after four and a half years, asking about Melody. Was it possible that he killed Gary? And if he were the killer, then surely his motive was all about Melody's wellbeing. To sum it all up, God forgive her, she would shed no tears over Gary's death- It was just one more assurance of Melody having a half- way decent future. If Lee-Roy did have a hand in it, she could find it, within herself to forgive him and even lend a helping hand if he needed it. For now, she rested in the fact that her baby was free from Satan's grip, or, so she thought.

MY GOD! DREAMS DO COME TRUE!

He was everything- Daddy, brother, friend, and mentor. He captivated her in a way that remained elusive to others and she believed he saw himself, through her ambitions. This unfamiliar love brought with it a clarity and direction to her otherwise struggle--fused life. Only problem was, he didn't know it.

When time permitted, Deborah and Curt would have lunch together in his office, or on the lake shore, near work. She found herself studying the shape of his lips when he was talking about her next assignment, or looking at his butt when he walked away. It didn't matter that she was twenty---five and he was forty---something, the fire in her pants was becoming unbearable and he was bound to catch a clue sooner or later.

Lately, they had been discussing the development of her own magazine. She had what it took to inspire people to action in a *full, color spread,* type of way. Unfortunately, he had to remain a mere consultant because the two jobs held a conflict of interests.

Deborah decided the magazine would be called *GRACE* because she knew only God could pull off the results of what she was hoping for. On this particular evening Curt was adamant about reviewing a list of graphic artists for the magazine layout. He knew the sooner they released the magazine the sooner they could expand into a television adaptation of its content. That's where his expertise would come in and he could leave corporate broadcasting for good. In Deborah's mind and in an alternate reality, they could live happily ever after.

It was eight thirty in the evening and Curt was calling for her to buzz him in. She opened the door to his disheveled, country boy charm, loaded down with briefcase in one hand, takeout in the other and a cell phone to his ear. He was telling Bernie to fax something over to the office while turning her dining table into a work station.

Once Curt got an idea in his head, he became a steamroller toward anything in his way. She watched as he pulled information on his laptop while they ate straight from the containers of Chinese food, but at that moment, she didn't care about layouts and top designers- She just wanted to kiss him. So, taking a gamble, she put down her food, stood up to get his attention, and then knelt down between his legs to kiss him.

At first, he sat there in shock, so she did it again and this time he held her face at eye-level drinking in her beauty and the possibilities. The length of his tongue provoked a skillful lust play that enraptured their senses. She had never had such a mature lover who understood the need for touch, and she allowed his hands to roam freely, touching all of her longing places. They disrobed quickly, unashamed of their nudity-voyeuristically taking it all in. Each, as difficult as it was, harnessed their appetite in lieu of taking their time with one another, exploring not only the orifices of flesh, but of mind and the elements that make souls cleave together. They were moldable clay in the palms of a certain thoroughness that would leave nothing untouched.

This indelible "love thing" carried on throughout the pregnancy, birth, and development of the magazine. They, by all means were parents and this growing media module was their love child.

The two of them celebrated rainy days like anniversaries. She distinctly remembered an April Shower when he lay betwixt her thighs, devouring all that lay between them. Curt, she noted, possessed a vigorous, skilled hunger that suckled on her nature to nurture. And she gave all she had. Her mind was no longer a single entity. It was entwined with his dreams and their creation. He, too, was inspired, and began calling in favors that would help them develop a cable network show. The format would be based on the magazines concept of, *change*. The brainchild went forth, picking up great ratings for a late night, newcomer. Their audience was growing; pushing them into the arena of success!

They soon purchased property that housed their enterprise, and took offices across the hall from one another. Deborah was so overwhelmed that she needed a personal assistant, of her own to keep up! Each one she hired seemed more incompetent than the last, until she demanded that the agency send her the absolute best candidate!

They acted quickly, and before long, a male candidate was there and ready to be interviewed.

"Well, show him in Rebecca," she told her secretary. And "in" he walked... Meticulously dressed, groomed, and well---mannered enough to wait for an invitation to be seated.

"Thank you for coming at such short notice. Please have a seat, Mr.?"

"Hammond," the gentleman answered. "Clive Hammond."

The name rang a resounding bell that caused Deborah to lock eyes with the gentleman seated across from her. She then tilted her head in amazement, realizing that it was her childhood friend, Lee-Roy Rodgers. "Oh my God!" She exclaimed in a baited, whisper. "As I live and breathe..." She got up to hug him and he allowed a brief embrace.

"From now on, I am Clive Hammond and you are Ms. Burrows. No exceptions. The past is dead to us- Am I clear?"

Deborah didn't know who she was talking to but was sure that remnants of Lee-Roy still remained, so she hired him for that reason alone. She knew Lee-Roy would never betray or manipulate her. She trusted him with her life and she could be trusted with his.

Without any further questions she extended her hand across the desk and said, "Congratulations, Mr. Hammond. You're hired."

WHITE CARPETS

The soft, white carpet tickled her bare back as Curt's flittering tongue tickled the tips of her nipples. At the same time, he firmly stroked her quivering vagina with his ever-ready penis, knowing that the combined sensation drove her wild! His own excitement was getting the best of him, causing him to stroke faster and faster, until she arched her back in total consent. The silver locket slid from her heaving chest to her arched shoulder. Using only his mouth, he placed it back in the center of her breast. She was abandoned to his pleasures and unashamed of how it appeared. "Harder!" She heard herself say! "Fuck me harder!"

Her handsome lover had no problem complying, he just continued to fuck and suck, feeling his balls slap into the crevice of her parted ass cheeks.

She was screaming, "I love you, baby!" when he stopped sucking her nipples and peered into her intoxicated gaze- "I love you too..."

Into his words, her body released a damned up flow of all the rejection, hurt, pain, and loss. A loud moan accompanied the release and she could feel his warm liquid squirting into her contracting vagina.

They had made the best love, ever, and she hated to see him getting dressed. But the truth be told, they never did make it home last night and decided to camp out on her office floor. Now, the sun was rising and Clive would soon arrive with coffee and those French pastries, she loved so much.

"What's on your agenda for today, Mr. Cavanaugh?"

"Well, honey lamb, I'm interviewing some boogie Brit, over lunch, to head our P. R. Department. He comes with high recommendations. You just stay here and play tea--party with your new girlfriend, Clive, and I'll see you tonight."

That was the first time she heard him make disparaging remarks about anyone outside of the political arena. She decided to ignore it, thinking his display of jealousy was cute. I could go with you. It might be fun. Then we could have a *"real"* lunch at Eataly! You love that place!"

"We're meeting over Rib Eyes, Darlin'. You are more than welcome to come, if you'd like."

"I'd *like*...

CAN I GET A WITNESS?

The meeting took place at downtowns', Atwood, a classy, Chicago favorite for business lunches that were meant to impress.

As they made their way to a corner booth, detailed with plush, velvet seating, and starched white cloths, she could see that their candidate was early. He awaited them with calm demeanor and smoke trails from an e cigarette. Furthermore, she surmised that he was *indeed,* boogie, reminding her of an urban James Bond with a tad bit of "street swagger." Deborah couldn't remember the last time she'd seen a white rosebud in the lapel of a man's jacket... Nor suspenders, a tie clip, and cuff links outside of Sunday service. The Clive Christian No.1 that wafted gently across the table spoke in volumes, stating that he was a man of taste- a man of style. He was so fine, she could almost hear her Aunt Vicky asking, "Can I get a witness?!" It was moments like these that she had to remind herself of how virile and sensitive of a lover Curt truly was.

As Richard Hawthorne stood to his full six feet, five inches to greet his new employers, he was immediately taken by Deborah Burrows sense of innocence. This subtle quality was not apparent to the untrained eye, but profiling people was his business. He found himself strangely doused with a need to protect his pedestaled princess, and before they even opened their mouths, he already decided to willingly submit his skills as the sword of her guardianship.

One at a time, Deborah and Curt shook the extended hand, tastefully jeweled in onyx and diamonds.

"You come highly recommended," Curt began. "What do you see for us?"

"You've originated from a solid concept, but you need to be rescued from obscurity, with a solid marketing strategy." Richard said plainly.

"Obscurity?" Curt countered.

"Rescued?" Followed Deborah.

"Yes. *Rescued from obscurity," he* repeated! You are popular in Chicago and some late night television spots. Your magazine is screaming for a cross-over audience..." Stopping in mid assessment- "You do want a syndicated brand, do you not?"

Curt and Deborah began to mentally explore the possibilities.

"Don't mistake my observation for something other than what it is. I know this is your baby, but we want the public to view this child as a substantial, credible news source."

Deborah noted that Richard had a way of explaining things that cut through the chase, yet was adept at avoiding main arteries. His manner was palatable for Curt who was rough and unwavering in his judgments.

"You," he continued, looking at Curt, "are a cut above average when it comes to investigative reporting and program management, but you lack the necessary people skills that build an unwavering trust in your product." Switching his gaze to Deborah--"You, on the other hand *are* a people person.

Deborah's wide smile quickly faded at his next words. "... But you are overly sympathetic to plights that don't further your cause as a whole. *GRACE* Media, no matter how humble its intentions, is a news source, not a melodramatic, docudrama. But your talents, combined will draw an audience that is waiting to be captivated by something genuine.."

The easy flow of his critique somehow lightened the blow. That, and the fact he was fishing the maraschino cherry from his Manhattan.

"...Which is exactly what we want, "Curt said, shaking his head with a new found appreciation- "Credibility!"

"So," piped in Deborah, "what do we have to do?'

"Does that mean I'm hired?"

Curt looked at Richard as though his poker hand had been exposed, and right then and there he folded. "Yes you're hired."

As the gentlemen shook hands, she felt like a queen snug in her fortress. All of them smiled, wide but none as deeply as Richard Hawthorn. For he had found the job that would restore his credibility, in the states and abroad.

Within six weeks of hiring Richard Hawthorne, publicists began hounding them for celebrity, spotlight interviews. As the press outlined their position, they were the *new brand* of stylized media! Sales grew to chart-topping highs and they now had European distribution! Richard suggested that Deborah, herself replace the host of GRACE Talk for a heart-felt edge against such hardcore news, but Curt didn't like the idea. She was print and he was television! The lines had been drawn in the sand since day one!

On the contrary, Deborah trusted Richard's judgment. He was quick to pick up on the needs of the enterprise and its consumers. He was an effective communicator and quickly remedied any negative fallout. Richard Hawthorne was worth his weight in gold!

YOU ARE NOT OPRAH!

"You're little boyfriend has you thinking that you're Oprah! Well, young lady, you are not! Stick tuh what ya know!" Tumbled Curt's hillbilly vernacular.

Deborah hadn't defended her choices since leaving Aunt Vicky and Uncle Bob. "I am a grown-ass woman, Curt Cavanaugh! And, I don't have a "*boy*" friend!"

"Sure ya do! I see the way you and Clive pass secret glances! He's not the most masculine stud in the world-But, hey- "Que Sera, Sera!"

"You are a pompous, jackass who swears that he knows everything!"

"Darlin' these eagle eyes and instincts have broken many a news story! Go check the mantle in my office. All those awards aren't just used to pretty-up the place! They validate twenty-plus years of success in this industry!"

Her mind caught, like bated breath because a part of her understood exactly where he was coming from. She had developed past the realms of his acceptance and understanding. Or, was it past the realms of his tolerance? When they'd met, remnants of Melody and the need for further molding, existed. But now, she'd become the person she always knew she could be, and the need for his tutorials on behavior were fading. It was a painful revelation that she had evolved into something other than his expectations. The same scenario played out several years earlier, when Aunt Vicky realized that she was turning down the scholarship and would not become a physician. And now, it was either she live in the shadows of Curt's limited idea of her, or face the results of her evolution.

"Personally, I don't see anything wrong with hosting my own show."

"Honey, there's more to it than sitting behind a desk in fancy clothes and blurting out responses! I'm just gonna be honest with you. How many successful, black talk show host are there?

"I'm not a statistic, or a color, or Oprah! I'm Deborah Burrows!"

"No! You're an idealist who doesn't play by the rules and calls your boot-strap luck, *blessings from God*!

She felt tears, well up in her eyes. "I thought we were like-minded in our beliefs...."

"Yeah, but Baby Girl, faith without works is dead!"

"So now, I don't work?"

"You float, Deborah-hoping by the grace of God that everything will land in its proper place!"

"And it has!"

"Because people with "know-how" make the impossible happen!"

"Maybe you're right," she conceded. "But we all have a part to play, and I have done my part and will keep doing it."

"Don't say I didn't try to warn you." His words were disturbingly calm. "I have to go away for a few days. A story I've been working on for ten years has broken."

"Where are you going?"

"Texas."

Right then and there, she knew things would never be the same.

FROM BULLSHIT TO BRITAN

Richards's secretary announced Deborah's arrival, via intercom. She didn't quite know why she was there or what she would say, but she did know that he was an adept problem solver.

When the office door swung open a well-dressed man smiled, nodded "hello" and left.

"Ahhh- Ms. Burrows, please come in." Richard said, smiling. "To what do I owe the pleasure?"

"Just wanted to stop by. I hadn't seen your office suite... Very tastefully done."

"Thank you. Shall I summon Margaret to bring you a latte?"

"No-no. I'm good." For a split second she drank in the way he just stood there, hands in pocket with the picturesque, Chicago skyline at his back. Curt had thought it only proper to give him a corner office suite, and she agreed. He belonged here.

"I just really need to hear you repeat that I'd make a good, morning show, host."

"Deborah, darling, I only say what I mean. And, if you'd like, I'll reiterate... You will bring your great big heart to a hurting world. And you will do it with class, and a style that is all your own!" He moved toward her, gently gripping each shoulder with strong hands only to look her in the eyes and say---"Trust your instincts. You can do all you've set out to do."

At that moment, she loved him because he confirmed *who* she was. It was such an emotional moment that she made a move she would regret for years to come--She kissed his lowered lips with a crimson stained pucker that lasted with lustful samplings. Surely, it was passion that caused him to enfold her in his arms, enveloping her body in such a way that she all but disappeared.

She was the doll he longed to play with as a boy. And he would have his time, even if, just for these stolen moments. Curt must never know how he secretly lusted for his brown, curly haired doll- And like Geppetto needed to see his creation live, he longed to see his Deborah walk in her *Queendom*---Even if it meant becoming her lover. Every touch of her orifices would represent the molding of clay.

It was "the making" that aroused his loins, and the finished creation that would cause violent orgasmic pleasure!

Deborah had no idea that she was in the process of being cosmetically crucified, but she subconsciously loved the pain.

After each love making session, a fitting followed. She was taught the silent statements made by Bulgari, Tiffany, and Cartier. Fragrance was to softly waft, not angrily offend. Hair, was now "coiffed" instead of "done" and crossed ankles were less threatening than crossed knees. They both had to laugh at that one!

The shows first airing, with her as the host started slow, but picked up steam when the topic of abuse was deeply explored and photos of a victim flashed across the screen. The sincerity of her concern was palpable and the live audience loved her!

Richard Hawthorne had created a million dollar potion and administered it, twice daily, via afternoon and late night television..

When ratings were revealed, corks began popping in celebration of GRACE MEDIA rising from obscurity! The air was clear and it was a time of great excitement. All Deborah wanted to do was share the electricity of the moment with Richard, but he was nowhere to be found. So, without so much as a phone call, she found herself outside of his Gold Coast, Brownstone, walking slowly, gingerly up to the front door. With every step, her mind snapped freeze---frame poses of their synchronized, sweat--drenched, love making. She was hot for those lean limbs to rap her and tap her, and enmesh her--"Ummmm..." she sighed. He must have anticipated her coming for there were rose petals leading up the stone stairway and trailing beneath the whitewood, double doors. A twist of the knob gave her easy access to the continuing trail that led up the stairs and into the master suite. It was at this point that Deborah realized Richard wasn't waiting for her, because the rose petal trail was now composed of discarded clothing, and noises, ever so faint, causing her eyes to pierce through the darkness. A man's form rose up in the moonlight to form a perfect silhouette. The figures continued thrusting, rhythmically, back and forth making faint noises that became grunts, impacted by ball-slapping thrusts!

"RICHARD!" She screamed.

Suddenly, the figures became as still as the air around them. Then there was a panicked shuffling, and Richard's British accent fighting through senseless excuses! A second voice that stunned and shamed her was asking, "Who the hell is she?!

In that moment her heart was breaking and her hands were shaking uncontrollably as she frantically searched the wall for a light switch to prove that her ears were deceiving her. She found it, but wished she hadn't... There, on the bed, sitting beside her lover was the man she bumped into, coming out of Richards's office.

She saw her towering lover stumbling as he tried to dress and run toward her at the same time. She heard him begging her to just let him explain!

"I love you, Deborah! It's just in a different way! Can't you see I was willing to suppress my own desires to make you happy? ...To create your dreams?" He was sobbing, but nothing made any since except to run. When her feet got the message they followed the specific instructions- *"RUN LIKE HELL*!" ...And she did.

THE MEAN TIME...

As days and weeks and months passed, Richard and Deborah licked their wounds and continued to work together, but never spoke of that night again.

In the meantime, traveling between Texas and Chicago, Curt was insisting on balancing the show with a more edgy "news" angle. At the same time, letting it be made known how disapproving he was of Deborah's sappy soap opera, morning show! The producers argued in favor of the current program and its packaging, while Curt brought new talent to the table in the form of blonde, bombshell, Phyllis Gordon. Despite her sex appeal, Gordon was a highly respected news columnist and commentator from California. It was said that she beheaded troublemakers with the tip of a pen! And then, there was Bill, a seasoned primetime producer who'd just been fired from a very reputable show. Curt wanted to make news and produce hard--breaking headlines, but Deborah wasn't sure that *Grace Media* was the forum for such a violent voice. They had become divided in their vision, and to make matters worse, Curt was willing to steamroll right over her to make this happen!

The board met on a Monday afternoon, in what they jokingly referred to as the oval office because this is where all executive decisions were made. By Monday evening the majority sided with Curt about a change in format for the now, popular, *GRACE MORNING SHOW.*

"Don't sweat it, honey," came Phyllis' throaty attempt at comfort- "Change is good. Besides, we're about to blow whistles on bastards from here to New Mexico!" Then she did what became known as, "the famous tawny, hair toss" which consisted of long, blond hair being tossed behind bared shoulders, and a runway walk departure.

I'M SORRY-MAYBE YOU CAN BE OPRAH

The evening found her walking down North Michigan Avenue trying to lose herself in the spirit of Christmas and the shoppers thereof. She had been built up and then crucified, in a matter of months by men she trusted. What was the price of a secure relationship, she wondered? The Next issue of *GRACE MAGAZINE* would be released in February with a focus on loving one's self. Maybe that was her answer- to focus on "self"- Maybe, take a trip and become aligned with her own strengths again. Her cell phone began to vibrate and looking at the caller ID made her hesitant to answer.

"What do you want, Curt?"

"To give you a chance to really be "OPRAH!""

"You were always rude, but never this cruel…"

"I'm not being either, right now. I need you to work, hand in hand with us on this breaking story…"

"Us?" Deborah responded. "You mean the plastic doll you found in Cali?"

"I don't have time for this bullshit darling'. Either you're in, or you're out. What's it gonna be?"

Deborah threw her head back, took a deep breath, and said- "I'm in." What she didn't feel was the chain on her silver locket, snap and her heart fall away.

*

The following morning, the floor manager was cuing her with the countdown to go live in--"Five, four, three, two, and…"

Looking directly into the camera, Deborah held an expression of serious empathy for her next guest.

"Good Morning. I'm Deborah Burrows, and you are watching *GRACE MEDIA MAGAZINE in the Morning.* "Today, we have the pleasure of expanding our Grace Media, family to include renowned news commentator, Phyllis Gordon, whom I know will bring a certain depth to the show. Please join *"us"* as we welcome our guest, victim of international sex trade ring, Abigail Nelson."

The camera pulls back to reveal the two women and their guest.

"Abigail, thank you for coming forward and sharing your story. Please, tell us how you were a victim of a sex trade operation for nearly eleven years?"

The twenty-eight year old, dark haired woman looked at Deborah as though she were confiding in a friend.

"It was Christmas Eve," she began- "I was just five years old, and my mother and step father had tucked me in for the night. I was in a hurry to get to sleep because there were tons of presents under the tree for me and I couldn't open them until morning. It seems that I had just dozed off when my step dad knocked on the door and told me to get up and get dressed quietly. I ask him why, and he said that Santa had hidden Mommy's special present down by the park, up under the tree I liked to climb. He said he needed me to go with him because he might get lost in the dark, and my mother wouldn't have a gift in the morning. So, quietly, I put on my clothes and slipped into my coat that he held for me, and we went to the car. When we got to the park, he kept on driving, even when I told him we were passing it up. He said that we were going to get ice cream first and then we would get the present. Hours must have passed, and I fell asleep. When I woke up, I was in an all-white room with white furniture, dressed in a white princess dress. A man and a woman came in and said that they were my new family and we would have a Christmas that I would never forget. They brought in food on silver trays and juice in wine glasses that tasted strong and different. My stomach felt funny and I asked to go to the bathroom. That's when I saw a port hole and discovered that I was on a boat. I demanded to go home! I screamed and I cried and I begged but they would not let me go. Days later, I was taken to a big house where there were many other girls and boys, and people spoke in different languages. All of us wore white and were challenged to keep our clothes clean. If we did not, we were beaten. The lady on the boat, whose named was Madam Hokku, taught us how to walk sexy, how to eat at the table, and to never argue with our guest-just give them whatever they wanted.

My first guest was a man that told me to call him John. I felt funny about that because I was only five years old. He would come by a lot and hold me on his lap while we talked. He would hold me in a way that I didn't quite miss home so much, and we would laugh... Every time he came I would look for these delicious chocolates that he kept in his pockets for me. When I searched for them it gave him so much pleasure... Every time he left I cried to go with him and he began to promise me that one day I would.

Six months passed and I was now six years old. This particular day, John came by, and was dressed so handsome in a gray overcoat and shiny shoes. He spoke to Madame Hoku in a soft tone, who then looked me up and down, and nodded. John handed her an envelope, she looked inside, smiled and told me to go and pack my things. John and I left hand in hand, stepping inside the chauffeur driven Bentley. Once inside, he said he had many things to show me and many things to share, but only if I called him Poppa. I gladly agreed, and this made him smile.

From then on, we did everything together, including sleep together. He said we didn't need our clothes because we had really warm covers and then he began touching me in places that made me feel good and bad at the same time. I hated him and loved him. He'd put his mouth on my privates and I had never felt such pleasure. My mind and body exploded. He brought me jewelry and lace handkerchiefs and perfume. We always dined at the finest restaurants and when people approached, he would tell them that I was his adopted daughter from the United States and they just said---"Oh, how darling..." In a year, or so I learned that I was in Milan, Italy, in the wealthy province of Basiglio. And by the age of thirteen, I completed finishing school in order to blend in with his high society friends, and also learned that John was actually Abele Di Gilio, a wealthy and respected banker.

As time passed, he would send me on trips abroad. I even went to New York a few times, with companions, on shopping trips. At the age of sixteen, he told me we could be married when I turned eighteen, but would have to move away because people wouldn't understand. I trusted him---He was my father and my friend!" At that point, Abigail began to cry...

As Phyllis patted her back and whispered words of encouragement, Deborah looked into the camera and said, "We'll be right back after this."-and they cut to a commercial break.

"You don't have to do this, Abigail." Came Deborah's strong supportive tone.

This caused Phyllis to jump up from her seat and lead Deborah to a corner, out of ear shot. "What do you mean, *She doesn't have to do this?*" Do you know what it took for her to come forward?! She can cry a river as long as it washes out the scum that takes little babies from their safe, warm beds! Her step father kidnapped and sold her to a flesh peddler on Christmas Eve, for God's sake! And the bastard is still doing it!"

Phyllis paused, and they both glanced at the floor manager who was giving the "thirty seconds to-air" signal.

"Grow some balls, Deborah! Real journalism is a tough, dirty business. You can use it to sugar coat shit or empower people!"

"And we are back, with guest, Abigail Nelson and cohost, Phyllis Gordon- Talking about, *Children, the Victims of Sex Trade*."

After Phyllis gave a brief recap for those just tuning in, Abigail continued...

"...I'd returned from Paris early- a trip Abele gave me for my sweet sixteen, birthday. Without anyone knowing, I slipped into the house and rushed to my room, changing into a red outfit with black, satin ribbons. My intention was to wait in his bed, making his breath catch at the sight of me. His car was due to pull up at any moment so I ran, quickly to his room and threw the covers back..." Taking a deep breath, she continued. "The little girl beneath them was startled and drew back from me! Her dark curls spilled over her naked shoulders in a million loops. Her brown eyes welled up with tears that began streaming down her soft, round cheeks... I picked her up in my arms and ran to my room thinking I had locked the door behind us." I dressed her and began to ask simple questions.

"How old are you?"

"Five years old," she said.

I was thankful that she spoke English.

"Where is your mom?"

She began to cry and said, "In Disneyland. I want my Mom," she sobbed. "We were going to ride the roller coaster and then the man came and took me to the car! I want to go home--please take me home, "she sobbed.

"Ok. I will. Tell me, where is the man who brought you here?"

"Right behind you love," came Abele's calm tone. Would you like to join us?"

"Stiff fingers of indignation and pain gripped my airway-I felt physically ill, like I would vomit and faint. My mind spun out of control, unable to comprehend the mutiny of my reasoning capacity. I never even realized that I had grabbed the cutting shears... I then spun around and stabbed my fiancée in the abdomen. I was still stabbing him when the evening maid came in to turn down the beds... The police were brought in and that's how I made it back to America

There were three seconds of dead air due to a stunned and saddened, Deborah. Phyllis stepped in to fill the gap while the Floor Manager was waving her hands wildly at a dazed Deborah. Finally, she took a deep breath, adjusted her poker face and cupped Abigail's hand with her own.

"Thank you for sharing your story. I can't imagine how difficult that must be to repeat. It is our understanding that you were given the proper evaluations and care that allowed you to live a healthy and normal life?"

"To some extent, I am able to live a healthy life. It will never be "normal". I was, however, reunited with my mother before she died, and I am married with a son and daughter of my own. ...Letting them out of my sight is sometimes a challenge for me. ...And I also compulsively check to see if they are in their rooms at night..." Her voice takes an eerie turn, trailing off with the thoughts that have haunted her throughout her return.

Deborah, who has recovered directs her attention to Phyllis...

"Phyllis Gordon and famed reporter, Curt Cavanaugh have been following this particular child sex trade ring for a number of years now. Can you tell us what you have uncovered, Phyllis?"

"Well, it started about fifteen years ago, in Texas. Children were disappearing from their homes, without a trace, during "bedtime" hours. It didn't seem to matter what neighborhood they lived in or what color they were, they would just disappear without a trace. The only connection these children shared is that they were all five years old. When the police were out of clues and the trail grew cold, the media attention would die as well and things would go back to normal, but I decided to write a piece, once a week concerning these missing kids and that is what got the attention of Curt Cavanaugh who began to investigate."

"And what did he find?"

"He discovered that every household that experienced a kidnapping had also incorporated a step parent into the home, within six months of the crime. It was his suspicion that the kidnappers were marrying into the family for the sole purpose of abducting the child. After the child had gone missing the spouse would stick around for a few months and then file for divorce, citing irreconcilable differences. Because of this discovery we now knew their target and could warn the single parent community.

"What about the overseas transport?"

"Because of Abigail coming forth with the boat information we were able to match the docking details with abduction dates. That trail led us to what appeared to be an orphanage in Turin, Italy, but what we suspect is an undercover *Baby Brothel*. ---A place where the over seer or Madame prepares the children for sexual encounters, and then introduces them to the physical aspect. But the most interesting factor of all, is that the facility is funded by a private group of philanthropist right here in the good ole U.S. Of A.! Investigations are underway and the children are being removed from that facility as we speak!"

VICKY COMES HOME

Vicky finally retired after working thirty years of night shifts at the V.A. Hospital. It was finally time to say goodbye. Bob needed her... Or was it that she needed him, to need her? Whatever the case, she wanted to be home. Unfortunately, after getting her wish, she couldn't seem to stay busy enough to match the measured pace of her nursing job. And the silence just about drove her mad. Today, she decided to give morning, talk shows a whirl. Whatever they were talking about had to be more interesting than waiting for dust to accumulate.

She turned on the television and froze as the talk show host moved across the screen. "No. It couldn't be..." she said out loud.

"Couldn't be, what?" Bob asked, on his way to the coffee maker.

All Vicky could do was point to the screen...

When Bob saw her, he froze too. "Is that our Melody?"

One hand went to her chest while the other wiped streaming tears. "Yes, Bob, that's our little girl..."

PART THREE

*Do We Really Reap What We Sow? And If
So, How Do We Survive It?*

SENATORS SLUMMING IT

After the show, Deborah didn't want to go home. She felt restless beneath the weight of the ugliest truth she'd ever heard. There was a cozy little pub two blocks south of her that had just the right amount of noise to drown out her thoughts. She chose a corner booth and ordered an Amaretto Cîroc. Secretly, she longed for Curt's company and some of his contagious inspiration. But, he was in Texas and things were still messy. The liquid "calm" was helping her to put her petty problems in proper perspective, and realize that there is a far greater purpose than the one she had originally supposed.

"Is this seat taken?"

Deborah couldn't help but smile, instantly reminded of that rainy day in the train station. Curt was smiling, too. "Have a seat, Boss Man. ...Thought you were out of town?"

"You think I would miss congratulating you? You did a great job. That wasn't an easy topic to deal with, but you handled it well"

"Thank you, Curt. And I have to agree, news like that really makes a difference in the world. Thanks for giving me a chance...."

"Ahhhh, there you are," said Phyllis Gordon in a flirty tone. Hope I'm not interrupting."

"No," Curt insisted! "We were just rehashing the show. You ready to go, Darlin'?"

It was the "Darlin'" that gave Deborah pause. She'd suspected that they *might* be screwing and now she knew. There was nothing she wanted more than to politely usher them out of her personal space, and she did, saying, "You guys have a great night." ...And by the way Curt slid out of the booth she knew that their night would be spectacular!

Nearly, an hour passed, and she was finishing her second drink. If she left now, she could maintain a sense of mild euphoria before the cocktail wore off, thus, achieving a peaceful slumber. Unfortunately, she would soon discover that *sweet dreams* were not in her near future... To the left of her sat a handsome, fifty-ish, white male, whose Testoni's and rigid posture indicated that this wasn't his crowd. Her eye for detail, told her that he was slumming it, and she wasn't going to stick around to find out why.

THE RICH MAN

The rich man took a long sip from his drink before addressing her…"Leaving so soon, Ms. Burrows?"

Not quite appreciating his familiarity, Deborah grimaced before responding… "Excuse me?"

"You, are Deborah Burrows," he said with confidence, " I know this because I watched your show this morning."

His creepiness was beginning to dissolve beneath a teasing smile. Deborah could tell that he found a wicked pleasure in knowing that he'd made her slightly uncomfortable.

"I can promise you that I don't bite, Ms. Burrows." He then rose from his seat with an extended hand… "I'm Senator, Jentezen Taylor, and you, my dear, need no introduction.

*

The argument taking place in Curt's office was heated. Deborah actually walked in on his administrative assistant ear hustling at the door. When she brushed past the woman and entered the office, a stillness fell…

Curt broke the silence by introducing the thin, curly haired man as, Attorney Vinson. "The man you see standing before you represents the conglomerate of flesh peddlers that stole Abigail's innocence! Flesh peddlers that the good lawyer here, refuses to name"

"Mr. Cavanaugh," said the man in a tsk, tsk, tsk tone--- "I do wish you would stop referring to my clients as "flesh peddlers". They are merely several individuals who thought they were investing in the wellbeing of others. Now, how this, Madame Hoku manipulated their good intentions into something so foul and inhumane, is anybody's guess, but you cannot possibly hold my clients responsible. I must insist that you stop this witch-hunt or you will be facing a mountain of injunctions!"

"If these people are so innocent then you've got nothing to worry about! And someone's child won't wake up after being drugged and raped in a foreign country, you greedy pig!"

"No need for name calling, Mr. Cavanaugh. Let's keep it civil."

Curt leaned in on his desk, so close he could see his breath move the curls resting on

Attorney Vinson's forehead. "Mr. Vinson, when I go to the supermarket and purchase a frozen chicken dinner, when I open it, I expect to see "chicken"; not beef or pork or shrimp... I expect chicken!"

"Your point being, Mr. Cavanaugh?"

"My point, Mr. Vinson is that your clients invested in an orphanage that is supposed to care for orphaned Italian children! Instead, this place is filled with terrified, abducted foreigners, who are being horribly abused and prostituted by a monstrous woman who calls herself, Madame Hoku! Now what I'm saying to you, Mr. Vinson, is that either your clients are dumb motherfuckers who don't care if they get what they pay for, or, they are getting exactly what they are paying for! And if that's the case, it's their turn to be terrified and fucked! Now if you wanna file injunctions, call the U.S. Attorney's office and see if they're interested in your bullshit! Cause as far as I'm concerned, you're just another pretty whore, gettin' pimped!"

Mr. Vinson removed his glasses and proceeds to clean them with his handkerchief. His demeanor being one of a silent, skilled hunter calibrating his rifle, and setting eyes on his prey. "Good day, Mr. Cavanaugh. I will see you soon."

"Good day, Vinson!"

Deborah waited until Mr. Vinson had left the room and exploded! "Why wasn't I told about this meeting? What are you, some lone gunman?"

"You have to realize, Dorothy-We aren't in Kansas anymore!"

"What the hell does that mean?"

"It means, do you think the people who finance this multi-million dollar, sleaze-fest are just gonna roll over and die?! We are in the big leagues now! No time for frilly panties and whatever lessons your fruity boyfriend taught you!"

Curt discerned that he had hit a nerve. "...Oh! You thought I didn't know about Richard?! You were fucking the stud in the office 'I' commissioned for him! Hell, you acted like a school girl on crack, when you met him!"

"My personal business is none of yours!"

"Sure, it is, Partner."

"We are partners only when you see fit! But, today when you confronted Mr. Vinson, my opinion nor my presence was even a consideration! You are a hypocrite!"

"No darlin'! I'm a realist!"

"Don't you dare call me "Darlin!" Isn't that reserved for your special piece?"

"I don't have time for your bullshit! Phyllis is an award winning journalist who is helping me gather facts to put these pieces of filth away!"

"And where do I fit in? I am a journalist too!"

"Oh my God! You call that night school crash course, journalism? Baby, we've been in the trenches, up close and personal with death! While you, on the other hand, put together cutesy pieces that unite neighbors!"

She couldn't move- couldn't combat his vicious attacks…. She turned to leave and suddenly he was behind her, penis hard, against her ass, hands groping everywhere- so fast and rough like a starving animal...

"I love you- always have. You left me" he said between panting... I have to keep you safe- you are the only thing that matters to me. Can't you see that?"

Somehow, she got loose and turned to face him. His breath was hot on her face- their lips, less than an inch apart. She looked at him and whispered ever so faintly,

"I am a grown-up- I am a person- I am worthy. You must learn to respect me..." She then twisted the knob in her palm, opened the door and backed out...

White Men "Can" Jump! They Just Use Private Planes...

What was she doing twenty thousand miles in the air with a man she only knew for three weeks? If the answer was "running" she would have to agree. Senator Taylor's plane was a luxury craft equipped with all the amenities and a butler to boot! She kept reaching for the chain that had helped calm her nerves through the years, only to be disappointed time and time again.

This man was funny, a good listener and attentive to her desires. But she was thirty years old and doubted if fifty five year old Jentezen could do anything to stir her passions. He was more like a father, slash friend that kept her mind and emotions in check.

Jentezen, however, had other ideas that he was careful to keep to himself. He knew she was young and beautiful and at many times inspired, but he needed her for his own plans. She must believe that she initiated the next level of this relationship or she might catch on too soon.

"Deborah, you are CEO of a powerful enterprise. *The pen is mightier than the sword, you* know. If you helped create this baby, you should damn well have a say in the way it functions! Now, I'm just an old dog, but I grew up under some of the greatest business minds in this country, and you've got to let it be known that you do exist."

Senator Taylor, I don't know how.

Reaching across the table, cupping her hands with his own, he said, ever so gently, "Let me show you *how.*"

*

It was late in the midnight hour and Curt hadn't even bothered with formalities, just sat pants-less on the leather sofa in his office, allowing Phyllis to go down on him. It wasn't necessarily because he wanted sex, as much as he wanted to not think about Deborah.

The phone was ringing, and in this silence it seemed louder than usual. Unwillingly, he got up, moving through the darkness to get to the phone.

"Hello."

It was Tracey, his Washington connection.

"Ok," said Curt---"bad news first."

"What you're dealing with is classified as a Matrix Structure- A complicated web of corporations where it's anybody's guess, who, is running what! It would be so easy for a CEO in Maine to pass the blame on to a subdivision that is conveniently run by Buddhist Monks in the Himalayas. Get my drift?

Curt sighed heavily. "Am I do to get kicked in the other ball, or do you have any good news for me?"

"The good news is, there are only a hand full of lawyers who are this good at setting up dummy corporations, and one of them works for a high powered political family in your home town."

Are you talking about, Big Daddy Mason in Texas; still buying and selling canned politics?"

"One in the same, my friend."

"Thanks Tracey. I owe you."

After hanging up, Curt grabbed a bottled water and sat his naked ass on the mahogany desktop. Phyllis got off her knees, pinned her hair back and reached for her laptop. No since fooling one another. They weren't going to sleep, or screw tonight.

*

BIG DADDYS HOUSE

Curt walked right up to the southern styled mansion and knocked on the front door. Again, he banged on the door like his life depended on it!

Finally, Missy opened the door, just as round and chocolate as she'd always been. She had smooth skin that dared you to guess her age and a way of causing one sentence to run on for miles.

"CURTIS," she yelled! "Come on in here boy and let me look at you! Aint seen you since you graduated from college and the judge threw you that big party! All the help was rootin' for your success! Sorry 'bout your mamma," she said sadly. "I visit her grave every time I go to see my mom up there at Burr Oaks.

"Oh, thank you, Missy. It sure is good to see you too," he smiled. I'm afraid this isn't a social visit. Is the judge around?"

In the distance, Curt heard the faint whirring of the Judges electric wheelchair.

"Missy, who in tar-nations was beating on the door like that?! Is everything ok?"

"Oh my goodness, yes! Look who's here, Judge Mason!"

The wheelchair came to a halt as the judge focused on his face. He couldn't yet tell if Judge Mason was aware of the investigations, and needed to weigh him out.

"Little Curtis Castillo from over on fifth street! Well, well, well! To what do I owe the pleasure?"

Curt was now convinced that the old coot *did* know, but was willing to play with him for a while to see what he knew. The old bastard was handing him a noose for the purpose of hanging himself. But what he didn't know, was that this old cowboy wasn't ready to die!"

"Hello Sir. Sorry 'bout all the ruckus, I just really needed to talk to you"

"Missy, pour us some of that bourbon, I like so much."

"No, sir. Non for me."

"Must be pretty serious, you giving up this Kentucky Sour Mash..."

"Must be pretty serious, you offering your old pool boy, the best in the house."

"Now, now Curtis. You know I've always treated you like a son. I put you through school and brought your mamma that house, over on Fifth Street."

"Seeing' as though you *ARE* my daddy, those aren't such grand gestures."

"What is it you want, Curtis?"

"I want to give you a chance to come clean about financing a sex trade operation that steels little girls and boys out of their beds at night for the purpose of servicing perverts!"

"What is this?! Some gallant, justice-seeking, gesture to avenge your mother's broken heart? Son," shaking his ancient head and staring through watery eyes-"that was a long, long time ago."

"Maybe the pain you caused my mother is what drives me, and makes it easier to call a spade a spade. All she talked about was how much she loved you and how you were going to marry her someday..."

"Curtis, that was a fairy tale from an old man who got a little friendly with the help. After all, I let her keep you and continue to work here, didn't I? Besides, your mother was a Spic! Can you imagine the scandal?"

Curt's expressions twisted beneath burning fury, and it was all he could do to keep from throwing his disabled father to the floor.

"I'm going to crucify you!"

"If you're busy digging one grave you might as well dig two. Damage control is under way, and trust me, you and that nigger-bitch you fuck, are no match for what's coming. Damage control is already in place!"

Curt kept walking past Missy who carried their bourbon on a silver tray...

"Curtis, don't you want your drink?"

Her submissiveness to that monster made him sick, still, he kept heal to dust, walking and never looked back.

*

The breeze off the Caribbean Sea kissed Deborah's skin as she stepped from Senator Harvey's plane and onto Martinique Island. She needed this piece of paradise like a drowning man needed air! She paused to drink in the clear water and white sands before descending the stairs.

Jentezen had made it clear that they had an hour to freshen up before dinner, cocktails, and dancing. ...And the answer to the nagging question in the back of her mind was, "Yes- I am running."

On the way to his room, Jentezen answered his cell phone wishing he hadn't. There was no introduction, just intrusion and disrespect.

"If you want to be reelected as Senator of Texas," the voice yelled-- "you won't screw this up, Taylor! My arms are still long and strong in Washington!"

Holding the receiver to his tense jaw, "You've made yourself abundantly clear, Judge Mason.

How long are you and my father going to make me pay for your perversions?!"

"You continuously threaten and disrespect this organization with your self-righteous judgements, " yelled the Judge!

"You must forgive me, sir," Jentezen countered calmly. I simply can't stomach a wrinkled, old man romance a child."

"I won't waste my time explaining something you will never understand! Now, you worry about keeping that porch monkey under control!

Everything is under control. Being with her, in public makes me very uncomfortable."

"Well, you are off in some god-forsaken island. That should help! It's no more than what you do for your other whores, anyway! Besides, if all goes as planned you won't have to do this much longer."

The judge hung up, and Jentezen just held the phone, wondering how much longer he had to string Deborah Burrows along.

Dining on the prawn and chicken curry, called Colombo, gave Deborah a new appreciation for island food. It was spicy and delicious, and at the risk of appearing greedy she ordered more. Jentezen just smiled and leaned back in his chair, watching her enjoy this experience. He found himself titillated by her excitement and later, he took her hand, leading her to the dance floor. As they began to dance to the island music, Deborah was thinking that he had pretty good moves for a white boy from Texas. Then again, so did Curt. She smiled and let the rhythm freely guide her dance.

Throughout the night the rum was flowing and loose lips began to sink strategically placed, ships.

"Tell me about yourself," Jentezen ask.

Feeling comfortable and safe, Deborah opened up for the first time in years about her life before GRACE MEDIA.

"I grew up in Chicago.

My mom died when I was six years old..."

Placing his hand over hers in a gesture of comfort... "I didn't mean to pry. You don't have to tell me."

"No- don't be silly. That was a long time ago. My aunt and uncle raised me, and wanted me to become a doctor. My aunt said it was a good profession because people never stop getting sick." She smiled at the memory. "I just didn't want that for myself"

"Oh- trust me, I do understand. I sometimes wonder how I got roped into politics," he laughed.

Deborah noted that it wasn't a happy laugh, but one that released frustration.

"Oh please! A United States Senator? You are responsible for making a difference in our lives. That is a beautiful thing." With those words she made eye contact with her most gracious host, and saw something within, soften...

"What are you doing here with me, anyway? Don't guys like you date beauty queens and throw private parties on yachts?"

"Oh, I have a yacht- We can do that next time, if you'd like. And, as far as being with you, it is because I want to be. You, my dear are a breath of fresh air."

Jentezen realized that he had learned in toward her face, and then immediately pulled back. What caused him further concern was that he was actually enjoying her company, her innocence, her truth. The later was nearly extinct in his world.

"Ok-enough of this!" He chided. Let's get some rest because tomorrow we go parasailing- Bet they don't do that in Chicago!"

"Well," said Deborah- "if they do, nobody ever invited me. So it's off to bed I go! Good night Senator Taylor," she blushed.

He stood as she departed, and watched her walk away. "Good night Ms. Burrows."

Senator Jentezen Taylor was in very big trouble because Senator Jentezen Taylor was falling in love with a target, scheduled for annihilation.

*

"You look amazingly tanned. Where have you been for the last three days?'

Deborah looked at Clive, trying to think of a convincing lie...

"Spill it, Ms. Burrows! We all know it's not Richard!" They both laugh loud and silly!

Deborah closed the door of her office. "You must promise to never tell a living soul!"

Clive's eyes grew large with disbelief. "Now, you know good and well that I can keep a secret! Who is he?"

"Senator Jentezen Taylor."

Clive's eyes grew twice as large! "Are you serious?! The House dreads him! You better be careful, my friend. Since when does he like black women?"

Deborah smiles. "Since he met me."

"It's an odd combination, Deborah. You hate to kill a fly, while he will shut down a factory, putting hundreds of people out of work!"

"Don't start, Lee-Roy!"

"I told you never to call me that!" The conversation ended when he walked out, slamming the door behind him.

They made love in the tropical hut to the sound of water, washing upon the sand. She'd allowed him to hold her and control their rhythm. The nail in his emotional coffin was when he'd lifted her up and eased her down onto his rock hard penis. She then put her arms, gracefully around his neck for support. The thought of her fit gripping his shaft made his breath catch, and with each stroke, they sighed in unison and never broke eye contact.

Later, when he held her close to his body, her head rested on his shoulder, and he knew he didn't have it in him to harm her. This thing was up close and personal, which is something he managed to avoid all of his synical life. He never even allowed himself to loved, nor touched in this manner. It made things messy prior to the chopping block. But, how, pray-tell, could he get out of this and meet the demands of Judge Mason and the powers that be? To go public with this love affair would be social and political suicide!

Laying there, bodies cupped together only covered by the gentle Caribbean breeze, he fought not to tell her the truth.

"You know, Debby, you should be with someone your own age. You are young and smart and beautiful."

She turned around kissing him with her full lips and then starred at him for a long. "Jentezen, you are perfect. You make me feel safe and secure." Then her head tilted to one side and she looked confused. "Do you have someone else? Is this just a fling for you?"

"Oh, my goodness, no! There is only you Debby" He kissed her passionately because the depth of his love drove him to do so. "You deserve better than me."

Yeah, right!" She laughed. "A handsome, U.S. Senator with a plane and a boat?!"

"There's more to life than titles and things."

"I know that, silly."

He had to make her hate him so much that she would leave and never look back! It would secretly kill him, but there was no other way. "Have you told your friends about us?"

"No."

"Why not?"

"Because we are so different... they will never understand."

He saw this as his chance. "If you love me, then they should only care about your happiness."

"I will tell them in time. For now I want you all to myself. And besides, I'm no fool Jentezen. Your family and friends will never accept us. That's why you fly me all the way to the Caribbean to be together."

"You are a smart one, Ms. Burrows. And yes, it's true, our relationship would not be received well." "Jentezen, you are just barely able to accept your feelings about us. We don't have to rush it. I'm happy the way we are."

He sat up and swept her into his lap. "Deborah, don't you know that you possess something very valuable? Your heart is pure and you still believe in people. Your GRACE MEDIA is a reflection of your heart, and it touches people in a way that changes them. What you do is good, he persisted."

She could hear something else beneath his words. Something he wanted to say but couldn't.

"Sometimes the gifts and power we have been given can rub people the wrong way. Very powerful people get upset and afraid that they might be exposed..."

"Jentezen, what are you talking about?"

He looked even more perplexed, like he might breakdown, and then his cell phone rang..."

"I'd better get that- Yes." He spoke into the phone. "Everything is under control. I'll be back tomorrow..."

Deborah never even gave his many phone calls much thought. That was a part of him that she wasn't ready to lay claim to. She was satisfied with what they had. Anything extra might rock the boat and make her face the reality of this situation.

Within two weeks Jentezen surprised her with access to his North-Shore penthouse. that faced the Chicago skyline. It felt like she'd come full circle, from being kept by Gary Williams in a luxury apartment to being kept a secret in a luxurious penthouse. Although It was eerily familiar, she felt comfortable enough to agree to the arrangement.

During their time together, Deborah began to open up about the investigation on the slave trade, never noticing how this was the only time he turned off his phone and did not budge. Jentezen was also becoming more and more obsessed with her movement and his frequent calls were becoming a distraction.

Simultaneously, Curt was receiving mysterious tips, clues, and hints on where to seek information, who to talk to, and what to ask. Apparently, there were enemies within the infra-structure willing to see this syndicate cave from the inside It would seem that the head puppeteer was a man by the name of Thomas Harvey, who amassed untold wealth through the family's lineage of boot-leg liquor and sex trafficking. Subsequently, he set up numerous small businesses, funded by the dirty money that grew into corporate assets. These corporations employed starving people in third world countries, who in turn were grateful to accommodate the hand that fed them.

Curt was furious, and continued to dig, but the trail grew cold until one day he received an old photograph with no return address. The people in the photograph were Thomas Harvey, Erwin Mason (his father) and a young boy, who looked painfully familiar. They were posing on the front porch of a rural cabin in clothing that could be dated around 1950.

He knew that Judge Mason was a scum bag, but would have preferred to believe his father had distant dealings with this operation.

Immediately he called Bernie… "Get me a plane, boat, or car to Pelican Hill off the Newport Coast in Cali!"

"No problem, boss man. But as you already know, this isn't your average community. How do you plan on getting in?"

Why darlin', I'm gonna walk right up to the front door. Hell, they already know I'm comin' It's a set up to see how much I know and how far I'll go! The only thing keeping me alive is the spec of good left in Judge Mason. But. If the truth be told, I wanna see this bastard, Harvey for myself, sweet cakes."

Ok-I'll text you the reservations. And stop calling me *"Sweet Cakes!"*

"Already done, Honey Buns!" Curt hung up the phone and took one more look at the photograph, before grabbing his jacket and shutting off the light.

RICH BASTARDS AND GOLF CLUBS

Curt's taxi pulled up to the guard shack of the gated community at ten am, and was allowed immediate access.

"Mr. Harvey has been expecting you," said the no nonsense, guard. There are four lanes, take the one to the far right."

Curt did as he was told, arriving in front of the massive mansion with a rigid butler who opened the car door and paid the cab driver.

"Right this way, Sir..." Leading him to a golf cart that transported him across the manicured lawns.

Within moments, the blur of a distant form was revealed as Thomas Harvey. It was a wonder that the eighty-two year old could lift the club, let alone, swing. The yellow sweater clad, gentleman handed the club to his Asian caddy and then turned to face him. He was tall with perfect posture and had no problem confronting him with piercing blue eyes, creased by crow's feet.

"Hello, Mr. Castillo."

"No one's called me by that name since college."

"To what do I owe the pleasure, Mr. Castillo?"

"You tell me? You're the one who lured me here."

"Nonsense! I've heard you were investigating some areas where I may have a common interest. It's only natural that you would show up here. I have lunch set up in the gazebo-Join me?"

"Sure. Lead the way."

As the waiter began serving their meal, Curt wasted no time *cutting through the chase.*

"Mr. Harvey, please tell me, why on earth a man of your means would steal children from their beds and carry them thousands of miles away from home to be raped by pedophiles?

" Sipping from his wine glass and savoring the flavor for a moment- "Because there was a demand for American children; specifically blond haired, blue-eyed children. Try your wine, while the temperature is still complimentary to the body..."

"A demand- For American *children*?" Curt repeated.

"Yes. *A demand*," he said calmly. "About forty years ago, give or take, there was a demand for Puerto Ricans. At that time we simply gave the parents a couple of hundred dollars, explaining that their children would have a much better life in our care. ...And, it was true. Those children were very well taken care of--- and loved, in a very special way..."

Curt had to stand up and walk a few yards away.

"What are you talking about?!"

"Your grandparents aren't dead, Curtis, like your mom told you. They are alive and well in an impoverished village in San Juan, Puerto Rico. We purchased your mother from them for your father, Judge Mason... Kind of a gift for being so helpful to the organization"

Watching the shades of horror and disgust on Curt's face evolve with each revolting word, Thomas continued.

"He was so taken with Eloisa's exotic beauty at just five years old, we set the adoption up and he had his little girl. At thirteen, she gave birth to you, and Thomas did whatever she wanted to keep her happy. That's how you lived your privileged life. But as years went on, she aged, and at sixteen she was just too old for him. So we used her to persuade the parents, in that village to give their children a better life also. It worked out well, until the demand changed. The Nouveau Riche started asking for niggers-go figure... Anyway, your mother just couldn't let things be and insisted on blowing the whistle if Thomas didn't stop giving little girls and boys a good home. This went on for years. He tried reasoning with her and she went on and on about having hidden letters, photos, and proof, until we just had to burn the house down to get rid of that sort of thing. We own the police, so no one questioned the fire or her death. You went off to college- a little sad, but you did ok."

The old man continued to drink his wine as Curt sank to the ground vomiting and grieving with silent, open mouthed cries. He couldn't catch his breath, even when the golf cart returned to pick them up.

"Will you be joining us, Mr. Castillo?" There was no answer. "No, I suppose not. You take your time and pull yourself together. Peter will see you back to the airport. And if I were you, I'd think about my poor old grandma and grandpa in Puerto Rico. So far they've been doing well, living off of our condolences. So don't tip the apple cart son."

With those words the golf cart rode away, carrying Satan back to hell.

Curt got back on a plane, but he wasn't headed to Chicago. He was headed to Texas to dig up the evidence his mother had planted for him.

Missy opened the door sobbing, barely able to talk. "You're too late!"

"Too late for what?"

"He's dead! Someone called on the phone with some news that upset him...- I never seen such a sight!- His skin turned pale,- his eyes went up in the back of his head, and he just slumped over! What are we gonna do, she sobbed?! What are we gonna do?"

"I don't know what you're gonna do about that old bastard! But right now, you're gonna tell me everything you know about my mother!"

Missy's eyes grew large as she backed away from Curt. "I don't know nothin'! Now you get out of here, disrespecting your daddy like that!"

Curt's eyes locked into her defeated gaze. "How'd you know he was my daddy?! How?" He took her by her mammoth shoulders and began shaking her!

"Alright! Turn me loose! I'll tell you! Your daddy had some wicked ways and folks was too afraid to do anything about it, seeing he was a judge and all. Lucky when I came I was already seventeen. He didn't want me, but the other help had to watch their kids around him, and them others when they'd come round."

"Missy, I need a list of every old codger that used to come here. And, another thing, did my mother have any girlfriends she used to talk to, or a special place she would go to get away?"

There was a Mr. Frank Rellis. He owned that factory that made street lights..."

"Yeah, Rellis Manufacturing- Go on."

"Well about the same time your momma came, Mr. Rellis adopted him a little Puerto Rican boy and named him Eric. He used to bring Eric around here all the time to play with Eloisa, and then we started noticing that Eric just wasn't the same no more..."

"What do you mean, not the same?"

"It just seemed like the light went out In his eyes and then he stopped coming."

"Does Rellis still live in town?"

"He has a house here, but his maid says he's in Florida most of the time. Eric still lives here. But before you go on that side of town you should be prayed up! He's on them drugs and other thangs."

"Missy, if some old freak raped you every day you'd be strung out too!"

"That's not true, Curtis. My stepfather had his way with me all the time. I never turned to drugs..."

Curt looked at Missy, stunned. He found himself hugging her just like he did when he left for college "I'm sorry for your pain. Thank you for helping me despite all you've been through." A tear ran down her face. "No. Thank "you", Curtis. Now hurry into town before it gets late. You'll find Eric by Mid--Town Park, on ninth. God be with you."

Missy closed the door and Curt knew he was on his own. The police weren't coming and neither would any household help, who witnessed these atrocities. Missy was right, he needed God to be with him.

WHAT'S A GIRL TO DO?

Mid-Town Park was brimming with the activity of everyday people, unlike on the hill of the wealthy. It was three weeks before Christmas and there was an excitement in the air. Clerks were patient and extra friendly. Children pointed at store window displays, and volunteer Santa's rang bells signifying the need for donations.

Curt began walking the length of the park looking for what Missy described as a strung out, indigent Latino. His eyes combed the parking lots, sidewalks and benches. Any man with tattered or outdated clothing was suspect. The search went on for hours, until he decided that coffee was the necessary fuel to keep this up. A lunch counter within the mall beckoned him to take a load off and a thin, yet aging waitress, smiled and took his order. Her dark, curly ponytail swayed to the rhythm of her walk as she returned with his fuel.

"You got all your shopping done?"

"No," answered Curt. "I'm afraid I'm here on business."

"Hold on! Hey, I know you! You're that news guy who used to be on WTEX," she smiled!- "I just knew it was gonna be my lucky day!"

Curt couldn't help smiling. "You've got a good memory. I haven't been on the air in Texas for over ten years.

"Some things you just don't forget."

"Well, maybe you can help me out."

"How so, darlin'?"

I'm looking for a man, around fifty five- sixty years old, Latino, goes by the name of Eric Rellis.

"The waitress's breathe caught, "What do you want with him?"

Curtis' discernment kicked in. "I need his help in a big way. I heard he was friends with my mother, a long time ago."

"Who was your mother?

"Eloisa Mason"

Something in her eyes conveyed terror. "I'm sorry, I cannot help you."

"If you know anybody who can- they'd be saving the lives of innocent children." He handed her his number and without drinking any coffee, left the counter.

"Wait!" She called out. "Meet me at nine o clock tonight, right here. I'll be off then, and we can talk.

"I'll be here."

*

Curt had time to kill and peace to make. He needed to talk to Deborah, because the treasure of who he was as a man, was hers to keep . She couldn't understand his ways, but none the less, he only wanted what was best for her, and now she was disappearing after the taping of each show. He took out his phone and dialed her number.

"Curt?"

"Yeah, it's me." Look, I didn't call to fight with you. I wanna make peace, because I know things didn't end well…"

Deborah was with Jentezen and felt so uncomfortable talking to him. "All is forgiven. We will talk tomorrow."

"Are you with someone?"

"We will talk tomorrow," she said and hung up…

Nine o clock was approaching causing him to run across Mid-Town Park to make it back to the diner on time. When he got there, the waitress was locking the security gate and waving "goodbye" to her co-workers.

"You wanna go back to the park," Curt offered?

"No." I hate that place! We can go to my apartment, if you don't mind?"

"Let's go."

Once inside the apartment, they both sat on the dated, plaid sofa in the meager surroundings. She grabbed a cigarette, lit it, and drew long and hard... "You got yourself in a mess, sweetheart."

"Does that mean you're gonna help me?"

"As much as I can. I owe it to your mamma."

"How do you know my mother?"

"We were friends. We were all each other hand, aside from you."

"I don't understand."

The waitress stood up. "Curtis, my name is Erica to the world, but to those who know me, my name is Eric Rellis-adopted son of Frank Rellis."

He then reached up and removed the ponytail, wig causing Curt's eyes to close and tilt his head backward. Then he stared for a long time before finally speaking.

"I need information from you in order to shut this operation down and put Thomas Harvey away!"

"I'd like nothing more than to see that happen... I know, by now you've experienced just how cold, that son-of-a-bitch can be! Daddy Rellis aint a cake-walk either!"

"I don't give a damn. With the right information, they're all going down, and you can believe that!"

"Well," Eric began, lighting another cigarette, "in the early-sixties, your mother and I were adopted from the same town by rich, white men who took us home like rag dolls. They dressed us up and gave us everything our hearts desired-But!" he annunciated roughly, "they could never give you enough to wipe out the memory of real love or your own mothers , sweet voice."

His hand went to the side of his head as if trying to hold onto what sanity was left.

"They would show us off like prancing poodles at parties and fundraisers. That's how I met your mother," he said, smiling at the memory. "While the adults hob-knobbed at the parties, we would run through those mansions, playing and singing until the wee hours of the morning. No one ever told us to stop, or to go to bed. We did whatever we wanted for as long as we wanted. Then, my new dad began giving me strange looks and wanting to hug and touch me all the time."

Eric's brow furrowed and his lips tightened." I resisted one time too many and he raped me by the pool. I screamed and hollered so loud that he punched me to shut me up. Hours later, I woke up to him attending my black eye and more fondling. Then he raped me again! I tried to run away and he locked me up! I never submitted, and continuously tried to run away. This infuriated him, so he beat me and loaned me out to the male guest at his parties! He hired teachers of the same persuasion, to home school me until I was ten, and thought to be under control. Only then did he allow me to go to school. That's when I was reunited with your mother at Mattson, the most prestigious elementary school in Texas... But then of course, you would know that, because you were amongst the privileged...". He laughs at the word "privileged".

"Let's get one thing straight, I'm on your side," Curt said with a no-none-sense tone. "I thought my mother was a maid who fell for her boss, until yesterday afternoon!"

"Please calm down, Curt. All of this is unearthing some awful memories."

"Go on," he sighed.

"While I was living a nightmare, your mother was convinced that she was living with prince charming. She kept saying how someday, Erwin Mason was going to marry her and she would own that big house on the hill. She spun that yarn all through Jr. High, until I almost believed her! Then one day she comes to me and says she must go away for a little while. I thought it was odd because graduation was in two months, but, true to her word, she left. Five years later, I see her walking in Mid-Town Park with a little boy, still beautiful but with no light in her eyes.

Curt wipes tears that won't seem to stop falling from his eyes. It is all that he can do to continue listening.

"She says to me, "I'd like you to meet my son, Curtis Castillo. He's the reason they sent me away.""

As our friendship rekindled, she shared that Judge Mason said it was best that people didn't know he was the father. It would look bad. He set her up in a house far away from the hill and payed her bills, while she traveled back and forth to Puerto Rico to recruit parents. In the meantime, someone had to look after you.

Curt looked at Eric with a mix of sorrow and surprise.

Yes. That's right... For two years I looked after you while your mother racked up frequent flyer miles to keep Big Daddy Mason happy. But things began to go terribly wrong, terribly fast. It was like Eloisa had an epiphany as to who she was, in relationship to this horrible business she was in. Her downfall came when she tried to get Daddy Mason to see the error of his wicked ways. When he wouldn't listen, she began compiling an impressive file of pictures, travel records, names, and dates; It took her years. During that time, I was a mess; tweaking on a number of drugs while battling sexuality issues... I distanced myself from you guys, especially when I joined the tranny scene. 'Bout time you were a sophomore in high school, I was a distant memory. Then I'd heard your mom was..." His voice trailed off, not wanting to speak of the tragedy.

Eric, my mother, although jaded, was a smart women. She must have anticipated that they would be watching her every move. I think she hid that file; the question is where?

Strange Bedfellows

As Clive passed a disheveled Curt in the hall, he mentally noted that he was back from one of his self-imposed missions looking even more manic than before. The vibration of his cell phone interrupted his thoughts, but the voice on the other end caused him to stand stark still.

"Billy? To what do I owe the pleasure?"

"This is not a social call, Preacher Boy! Your boss done stepped in some hot shit and it's about to go down!"

"Can you meet me in an hour?" Came Clive's steady tone.

"Done!"

Within an hour the two men sat across from one another in Clive's office. The atmosphere was heavy with the weight of impending danger.

"Everybody, who's anybody is all up in arms about Senator Jentezen Taylor marrying your black boss..."

Clive jumps to his feet, exasperated and offended by the racial innuendo! "Billy, not you too!"

Billy, never losing his cool, "Me too," what?! Surely you're not naïve enough to think that this merger is about *true love*, are you?"

"Why not?!" Clive asked, feeling a bit defeated. When he knew full well that Billy's words bore an unnerving witness to Curt's sentiment...

"Wake up, Preacher! My parents and their country club cronies have been talking about Jentezen's, quote---unquote *"situation"* for some time now. And they aren't using terms like "Match made in heaven" or, "Fortunate pair". Instead, they are throwing around words like "purpose" and "agenda". And my personal favorite, *"What on earth?!"*.

Clive's gaze turned from Billy as he slowly shook his head in a pendulum-like disbelief.

"I see that you're beginning to hear me now. That's only the tip of the iceberg, son. Every now and then, when I need to get away I go hang out with my boy, Tommy. Tommy is an old cat who stays with his woman and her kids over in the   Linda V. Grails Housing Projects..."

Clive knew the place well because his father, Reverend Rodgers insisted on winning souls in the heart of the dope dealing, gun toting ghetto! The memory made him sweat.

"...But before that," Billy continued, " Tommy lived in Texas and made a living smuggling little girls and boys across international territory. The men who paid him said they were abused kids going to people who would care properly for them."

"Billy, this story is creepy and strangely intriguing but what in the Sam hell does it have to do with Deborah and Jentezen Taylor?!"

"Oh, I'm getting there, Preacher Boy! These kids were being abducted, trained as sub-missives and sold to filthy rich perverts under the guise of adoption. Now, it would seem that the group of men who finance, and prosper from this sex trade ring, approached my grandfather many years ago, inviting him to join..."

"And?!"

"Well," Billy said, sitting back and pulling out a hand rolled cigarette. " My granddaddy told me that he excused himself from the room and came back aiming a shotgun. He told them that if he ever caught them in the state of Illinois again he would blow them back to Texas! All ability to reason fell by the wayside as those bastards high-tailed it out of there!"

Billy chuckled and proceeded to violate the *no smoking* policy. "Those men were billionaire, Thomas Harvey and Judge Erwin Mason."

Coughing and fanning away second hand smoke, Clive somehow managed sarcasm by nodding his head and saying, "Thank you for a history lesson on our nations perverts!"

"Preacher Boy, few people know it, but Thomas Harvey is Senator Jentezen Taylor's daddy.

And Judge Erwin Mason is Curt Cavanaugh's daddy."

"That son-ova-bitch!" Clive yelled while storming out the door. Bernadine appeared from her office to see what all the fuss was about and catch sight of the ruggedly handsome, Billy running behind a hell bent Clive!

"Man, slow down! YOU DON'T KNOW EVERYTHING!"

"I know enough!"

Bernadine was speed dialing Curt who came around the corner, saying, "Here I am Bernie" and then collided with Clive, who grabbed him by his tattered t shirt!

Curt shoved Clive into the adjacent wall and then stood shirtless watching some white misfit trying to subdue and calm Deborah's wiry assistant.

"Look, I don't know what you're on," giving Billy the once-over, "or into, but I will kick your frail ass from here to Mississippi! I've had enough of this! I'm gonna talk to Deborah about replacing you!

"If you go near Deborah, I will hire a hitman! I know all about your sex tradin' daddy!

Curt froze in his haggard tracks, not knowing if he should get his pistol or get a location on Deborah. He chose the latter.

"Bernie, get Deborah on the phone for me. And, Renegade Dude, bring this fool into my office!

Curt took a seat on his desk, Billy perched on the arm of the sofa and Clive paced frantically!

"Who are you, and why are you in my building?"

"My name is Billy Westinghouse, and I'm here because Preacher Boy's friend is in trouble."

"Who the hell is Preacher *Boy?*"

"This man," tilting his head toward Clive. "Wearing a hole in your carpet!"

"Ok," Curt dismissed, "we will deal with that later. What is it you think you know about my father?

"That he's a flesh peddlin' pedophile and the apple don't fall far from the tree!"

"Preacher Boy, Curt is not the enemy! Thomas Harvey is!"

"Now we're getting somewhere,"   came Curt's response.

"Thomas Harvey," continued Billy "inserted his son into Deborah's life to keep an eye on how close Curt was getting to the truth, and to also acquire stock in this enterprise. And judging from Deborah's broadcast,   Curt has uncovered quite a bit."

"Hold on! Thomas Harvey's son?"

Clive, finally able to assimilate the information sat down and said in a calm voice, "Senator Jentezen Taylor is Thomas Harvey's son. Curt, you were right all along."

"I'll pat myself on the back later," Curt said, as his mind flashed back to the two men and the young boy in the photograph. It clicked that the young boy on the porch was Jentezen!"

That's when, one at a time, the gentleman took turns sharing all that they knew. Clive came clean about his true identity and why an alias was necessary. Curt revealed his search for the documents left behind by his mother, and Billy Westinghouse volunteered his service to shut this operation down!

The Bird In The Hand

She was exhausted. Beads of sweat rolled down her forehead and chest. Her nipples stood erect, kissed by the Caribbean Breeze. He looked like Jentezen but the intensity of his love play spoke in tones of desperation and fear. The latter was deciphered by his need to cleave tight to her sexually battered body in a bone--to- bone fashion. What, pray-tell, was he so afraid of?

Exiting the lanai she went into the bathroom allowing gentle streams from the five shower heads to ease away her soreness. Afterwards she guzzled a papaya juice straight from the bottle, and took in her beautiful surroundings. Her eyes came to rest on a nearby table in the corner of the room that was strewn with papers, a passport and what appeared to be photographs. This mess was so unlike Jentezen that she felt compelled to straighten up. Deborah went down on her hands and knees, sweeping one hand beneath the sofa to fish for stray papers. What she found, instead was something small, hard and cool to the touch. When she pulled it into the light her breath caught with joy, confusion, and finally, rage! What she held in her hand was the beloved locket, lost all those months ago.

Her phone began to vibrate on the counter, near the mini bar. The stillness of the Caribbean night made the noise seem deafening. She saw that Curt was calling, then Clive, now Bernadine! She shut them down and headed for the lanai to confront Jentezen.

"Wake up!" Deborah shouted. "Wake up!"

Jentezen sprang forward, unable to focus on the source of alarm!

He called her name in a startled yet concerned tone- "Deborah! Darling, what's wrong?"

Slowly, Jentezen calmed and began to focus, not so much on Deborah's blurred form, but the object dangling from her uplifted hand. He quickly discerned that she was holding the locket that slipped from her neck and fell to the sidewalk, so many months ago. He'd been stalking her as ordered by Erwin Mason and his madman of a father, Thomas Harvey. And now, here he sat, exposed. He could lie, protecting the organization and his political career, or he could admit that up until six months ago, he was a ruthless bigot whose only mission was to crush her like a cockroach. Truth be told, he still wouldn't live amongst Mexicans!

"Well, I'm waiting?

" I was following you the day you interviewed Abigail Nelson. The locket dropped from your person as you walked, and I picked it up..."

Deborah, infuriated, countered, "And you had it all this time and never returned it? This locket is all I have left to remember my mother by! What is your problem?! Who are you, really?"

Rising from the day bed and reaching to comfort Deborah only made things worse.

"Don't touch me Jentezen! You are going to sit down and start from the very beginning!"

"Deborah, I really don't want to lose you. And the truth will destroy us!"

The phone in her robe pocket began vibrating. She pulled it out knowing that the frequency and urgency of the calls held the answers Jentezen was trying to avoid.

Jentezen knew it too as he held her eyes with a gaze that begged her not to answer.

"What's the problem Clive?" She said calmly. "Don't you know it's three o clock in morning, here?"

As Clive began giving the abridged version of their plight, the impact was evidenced by the locket being lowered to her side.

It was Jentezen who broke the gaze and reached for his phone. She could hear him through the haze of her brokenness, waking the pilot for their impromptu departure.

During the flight not a word was spoken between them. And it seemed, not until they touched ground and she beheld Curt, Clive, and Billy that she could breathe again.

ROUND TABLE WORKOUT!

Back at GRACE ENTERPRISES, the five of them sat at the conference table, each man on the brink of his own explosion!

"If it means anything," Jentezen ventured, "I do love Deborah..."

Clive's fist hit the table so hard the sound resounded throughout the large room! "You don't get to talk about love! Your dad is the devil and you are his punk-ass minion!"

"Now!" Tumbled Curt's eerily calm, country accent. "What's Daddy Harvey's next move?"

Jentezen rose from the table, turning his back on the pack of persecutors, and walked, casually to the wall of windows.

"Gentleman, I don't think you realize that I'm here because I choose to be here. I could have had my pilot fly us anywhere in this world, and made Deborah disappear forever..."

All were silent, except Billy. "But you're sick of your daddy runnin' your life," pausing in mid revelation. "...aren't you?!"

Jentezen, in his fifteen hundred dollar shoes turned to face Billy in his worn out sneakers- "Yes, I am."

"Well, son, today is the day you become a man."

Jentezen Taylor nodded, sat down and began explaining how a twenty---three year old corporate climbing, Thomas Harvey had an affair with his thirteen year old mother in the early fifties, and she became pregnant with his child.

"Despite repeated requests and threats for her to have an abortion, she ran away to Virginia and gave birth to me."

If one didn't know better they would have detected notes of melancholy in his otherwise, austere tone.

"However, Thomas Harvey paid my mother's best friend to betray her and she did by notifying Thomas that he had a son. But a bastard son by a minor wasn't a good look for Corporate America. Therefore, he paid a struggling law student , by the name of Patrick Taylor Sr. a handsome sum to marry my mother when she turned sixteen. Needless to say, he took the money and the servitude that came with it. Those were my father's first experiences with buying people. It turned out that

Patrick Taylor Sr. was a brilliant investment who went on to chair deals between Thomas and some of the world's wealthiest and most influential people. So you see, the roots of this underground organization run long, strong, and deep."

Curt looked at Clive in an "I told you so" manner, who closed his eyes and shook his head.

"When I was twelve years old," Jentezen continued, " my daddy told me we were going to Tennessee on a fishing trip. I thought it was strange because Patrick Taylor Sr. never ate dinner with me, let alone have "father and son" time! When we got there, sitting on the front porch were Erwin Mason and Thomas Harvey. Thomas took me by my shoulders, looked into my eyes and said,

"Say hello to your daddy!"

"It was at that point that Patrick Taylor Sr. Told us to turn and smile for the camera." Looking at Curt, "That is the photograph that I had anonymously delivered to your office."

Deborah tilted her head to one side. "What photograph? You mean to tell me you've been keeping things from me?

"I wanted to protect you."

" So do I, " said Jentezen in a tone that left no room for doubt. " I was trained by some of the most brilliant business minds, ever born. And every one of them enjoys the smell of fresh meat, which drives them to kill.

"Well, apparently there is a file, that was compiled by my mother against Judge Mason. Do you know anything about this file?

Jentezen peered off into the distance, accessing mental files. "...Oh yes," he sighs... Your mother, Eloisa. ...The era in which the organization aided in adopting Latina children. I met her when she was about twelve years old. A real beauty, she was... But, I digress... There were many files, but quite honestly, I can't think of one associated with Eloisa. But I do recall buried files detailing the disappearance of drug-runner, Gary Williams."

Everyone in the room witnessed Deborah and Clive go ghostly pale and fall off into the background.

"Now, Deborah and Clive," came Curt's serious tone, " I'm sure we'll work our way around to your nefarious deeds, but for now, let's stay focused, shall we? My mother was brokering deals for the sale of children to Thomas Harvey's pedophiliac buddies. This went on   for years! When she couldn't stomach it anymore, he killed her! But not before she compiled a file on the operation!"

"Not to be insensitive, Curtis, but the way I understand it, there was a fire that destroyed everything, including her accusations."

Curt swallowed hard, fighting the lumps of indignation and pain, rising up in his throat. "Jentezen, are you here to help us, or hinder us?"

"That's what I wanna know," Clive said roughly! Do you know about the sex trafficking, or not?!"

"Somewhat... Never had the stomach for that end of the business. A weakness my father spent years trying to correct."

"Jentezen, just tell us what you know," Deborah said wearily.

"I know that what you're looking for isn't in a file. I also know that 'Madame Hoku' isn't just a name, it's a 'title'. There are hundreds of Madame Hoku's stationed across the world! And you, my friend have already made contact with one of them. You, indeed, had your file right in front of you and didn't have a clue! You must think, Curtis Castillo!"

Without warning, Clive leaped across the conference table, grabbing Jentezen by his tailor--made collar! "You son of a bitch- stop playing games!"

Jentezen laughed, a loud inappropriate laugh that caused everyone to pause.

"Come now... I am a monster, just like my mentor. But I am a monster in love. My loyalty is to Deborah-not this group of amateur detectives!"

Billy Westinghouse had slipped out of the office and into the quest of finding breadcrumb clues left by Curt. He knew time was of the essence since Jentezen had slipped off the organization's grid.

Deborah's eyes widened in horror, not believing that a mere eight hours ago this man lay betwixt her thighs and inside her nurturing womanhood. "Why didn't they just kill us," she heard herself ask?

"There is an unbreakable rule that states, 'we can do no harm to family. If you become my wife that rule would apply to you, as well. You would be safe!"

"So the rule applies to Curt too?" Sighed a relieved Deborah.

"Not anymore. When Erwin Mason died and Curt ignored the warnings of Thomas Harvey, he was viewed as an enemy, due for termination. You should of left things alone!"

The room grew still as they absorbed the meaning of his words. *"Curt was a target..."*

LURKING IN THE SHADOWS

Watching the show from a dark, rear corner gave Billy the perspective he needed to put this puzzle together. He discovered that by day, she was a middle aged waitress, working in the park district. By night, she was the *tranny with the big round fanny,* shaking it for the underground scene!

The only thing more obscene was how Erica lied to a bewildered Curt about her relationship with Eloisa. His new friend was too close and too wounded to be objective.

Billy, however, was keenly objective, tracing Curt's steps to the last connecting factor between Eloisa and Thomas Harvey. Hence, the *living file* referred to by Jentezen. Yes, Billy observed, a walking talking ledger of all that took place during the 1960s sex trade operations.

When he arrived in town he followed Erica from the diner to a shady night club. There, he spied on her from the shadows, watching as she transformed into a naughty vixen for the male dominated crowd. The atmosphere was eerily lewd, the people anatomically restructured, and the perversions were not for the weak of heart.

While applying the crimson lipstick her cell phone began vibrating on the vanity table. Without missing a stroke she answered the call.

"For the tenth time, I already told you, he doesn't know a damn thing! I kept my end of the bargain! I hated the little bastard then and he's still a pain in my ass now!"

Slamming the phone down on the vanity table, she stood up and blew drug induced kisses at her reflection. It was now time to hit the stage and from what Billy heard, she was the highlight of the evening. The applauds always led her to a celebratory line of blow, and a hot bath. This evening would have been no different if there wasn't a young, beautiful man peering into her dressing room.

Bowing her head at the glass alter of blow, she arose refreshed and confident. "Won't you come in, dear; tell Erica your name?"

"My name is Billy and I'd like to spend some time with you."

Billy Westinghouse Is a Bad Boy

Billy found himself at Eric's house accepting a drink and what he was sure was the best seat in the house; a yellow, leather recliner complete with duck--tape repairs. As he waited for his host to change into something more comfortable he tried to view this scenario through Curt's eyes.

"Here we are," came the drug induced pitch of a lace clad, drag queen. "Can I freshen your drink?"

Billy's eyes followed his flittering host all over the room until she perched on the adjacent plaid sofa. "No thank you. I've barely touched this one."

"Perhaps there's something else you're thirsting for?" Erica said in a no non-sense tone.

"You are very perceptive, Billy smiled."

Without another word, Erica rose from her perch as graceful as any six and a half foot drag queen could, and dropped to her knees between Billy's legs. As the Crimson nails crept up his trousers for the unleashing of his junk, he grabbed her ponytail, snatching her face into an upturned position! One punch was enough to send blood splatter in every direction and render her a helpless mess! The weight of her shocked body slumped over, on the worn, beige carpet with a loud thud!

First there was gasping, and then a baritone voice offering Billy money and jewels hidden behind the toilet tank.

"I don't want your money, son."

This seemed to frighten Erica even more. "Then what do you want?"

"Names, dates, locations."

Erica's eyes widened. "Of what?! I don't understand!"

Billy looked around and then ripped an edge from the lace table cloth, throwing it at, what he considered a quivering mass of wasted masculinity. "Clean your face and we can talk as men."

Erica grasp the cloth like a defeated child, pressing it to her bleeding nostrils. "Please just tell me what you want! I'll give it to you!"

Suddenly, there was a knock at the door and Erica began yelling out- "Help! Someone help me please!"

It baffled her terrified mind, further when Billy strolled to the door and unlocked it. In walked Lil, Curt Castillo to whom he silently pleaded with confused eyes... "Curt, I don't know what's happening, but please tell this young man that

I wouldn't hurt a fly! I have loved you since you were a boy!"

The next man to enter caused Erica's breath to catch, and a stream of urine to saturate the area of carpet on which he sat. Finding breath, he managed to sob- "Oh my God, Senator Taylor please don't kill me! You all made me set the fire! I did what you told me! But as you can see, Curtis lived... Per Mr. Harvey's request! He said if I helped then I would be taken care of, and I helped! Please don't kill me!"

Curtis eyes filled with tears as he spoke slow and deliberate.

"We are not going to deal with that right now. All we want is enough proof to connect Thomas Harvey to the sex trade operation!"

"What are you talking about? You've got bitches on tv testifying about their own kidnapping and captivity! You know all about the sexcapades! What else do you need?!"

"I need this motherfucker to crash and burn!"

Erica sat up, discarding the bloody cloth on top of a nearby crate, slash, end table. "The truth is, that Eloisa and I did reconnect in the park district when you were just five years old, but it wasn't by chance. I was sent to spy on her. The powers that be, made it plain that this wasn't a job I could turn down. Furthermore, I was too old and used up to be a boy toy, plus, I knew too much for them to just let me go. So, they put me to work as your mothers babysitter and confidant. They paid me in drugs and promises."

"I'm more interested in what my mother had on Judge Mason that made him kill her!"

Erica took a deep breath. "Judge Mason invited your mother over for dinner one night, telling her it was in celebration of the great job she'd been doing in Puerto Rico. However, in her mind, she believed that he had come to his senses and finally wanted to become a family. As the evening progressed, the judge began to talk about her being promoted to a position of authority and respect; how she would have a new title and live in a big mansion, much like his own.

She told me, that as his eyes lit up with excitement, hers peered through his story for any signs of a "happily ever after". She soon learned that there wasn't going to be one.

"Yes," came Erwin's easy, yet authoritative tone- "you will have a huge estate in Puerto Rico, with servants and administrative staff. I, of course will come out to see you, every now and again to make sure everything is running properly, but you, my dear, will be in charge."

"Administrative staff? In charge? What are we talking about? I don't want to live in Puerto Rico! What about our son?" She pleaded. "What about us?!"

Erwin sat back in his chair, shaking his head as if he couldn't believe the stupidity! "I'm offering you the world! When are you going to give up this fantasy about us?! There is no, US!"

"But why, Erwin, she sobbed? You used to love me…"

This last statement was spoken in a manner that expressed irreparable defeat.

"Eloisa, it's true. At one time you were my pride and joy… So innocent, and wondering what life held around every corner. Now, there is no more innocence! And your young body was totally defiled by giving birth. I could never desire you in that special way again!"

He is our son!"

"And I swear by this organization, that as long as I'm alive I will take care of him, just as I'm trying to do for you. Now there will be a top secret and heavily guarded meeting detailing your new life, on tomorrow evening. Someone will pick you up from your house at seven pm. Just get in the car and go. No questions; understood?"

Eloisa shook her head, realizing that Edwin Mason had no other interest in her, besides business, and that's when she set out to destroy him.

WHAT THE HELL HAPPENED TO
GARY WILLIAMS?

"Please tell me that you and that strange white boy didn't kill Gary Williams!" Said Deborah.

Clive snatched Deborah by the arm to the tune of raised eyebrows, and pulled her into an empty office suite.

" Don't you dare talk to me about *strange white boys*!"

"Answer the question, Lee-Roy!"

"Pointing his finger directly in her face. "I told you to never call me that! Are you crazy?!"

"What your name is, is the least of our worries! Now, did you kill Gary?"

"Not exactly..."

Just when he thought Deborah's eyes couldn't get any larger, he was wrong, but it was the slump in her shoulders that made him start talking.

"Deborah, it was in self-defense...."

Deborah sat down on the floor, back against the wall, wanting to know, and *not* wanting to know, at the same time.

"One of the reasons no one knew where I was after my release date is because I was stalking you and Gary."

The look on her face saddened him so deeply that he felt tears well up in his eyes, yet he continued. "I saw what you didn't see. The women, the drug deals, the wedding…."

Deborah tried to repeat the word *"wedding"* but could not. Her only solace was throwing her head back, allowing the tears to roll silently down her face. At this moment in time, they were kids again, tucked away in Reverend Rodgers study. It was safe to cry.

"One night, 'bout one am, Billy wanted to ride shotgun on my mission, which of course, was tailing Gary. We followed him from Brookfield, Illinois, all the way to the South Shore of Chicago. He got out of the car talking to someone on his cell phone and started walking toward a high-rise building. He was so engaged in conversation that he didn't hear me walk up behind him. When I tapped him on the shoulder, he spun around and acted as if he'd seen a ghost! And then he realized that it was *just*," raising fingers in quote, unquote signification, "Lee-Roy Rodgers!"

"He started towards me and put his arm around my shoulder, tightening the grip for a headlock. When I slipped away he became furious!"

"It's been awhile, faggot! I see you got out of them high---water pants; lookin' like you were always ready for a flood! Boy your pants would of never got wet," laughing wildly!

Billy emerged from the distance. "Preacher Boy, why don't you let me handle this one? You go and rest on one of those rocks; watch the sun rise."

Gary tilted his head to one side, recognizing Billy as the renowned street legend. "I know you! What you doing down this way?"

"I'm a humanitarian, Son! I go wherever there's a need. Preacher Boy don't seem to need me, so I'll just sit down, over on the rocks.

With confirmation that he would only be dealing with one of them, Gary proceeded to advance upon the Lee-Roy Rodgers, he used to know. With every step he took, he swung at Lee-Roy, who backed up and dodged the blow Billy, who had tired of this dog and pony show, pulled tobacco from his jacket pocket and began rolling a cigarette.

"PREACHER! It's time to stop running! Hit that fool, so we can go home!"

"Naw! What we got here is a grade A pussy who wanted to fuck Melody, but is just as much bitch as she is! Now' you got a chip on your shoulder cause I fucked her?!

Lee-Roy, who masterfully, bobbed and weaved also had to accept that there very well, may be some truth to what Gary was saying.

He had been afraid. He had been a pussy, and as awkward as it felt, he had fantasized about making love with Melody Baxter... But of all the bastards in all of this entire world, who the fuck was he to judge?!

Lee-Roy Rodgers, in that moment, transitioned into the man he always wanted to be and knocked Gary Williams, the fuck out! Billy leaped up from the rock on which he had been sitting, holding his arms in the field goal position!

"Can we get a burger now? I'm starving!"

Walking to the car, they both heard the click of the gun, but Billy was faster on the trigger than Gary...

Before entering the car, Eloisa was blindfolded and then silently driven, what she estimated to be eight hours away. Her and the driver then walked through trees and crackling leaves until they came upon a shack with a broken down sofa on the front porch. She just knew this was a *"don't judge a book by its cover"* situation and things would get better once inside. That wasn't the case. Several young women, of various cultures and colors sat on dilapidated furnishings, giving her the once-over and then turning their attention back to the woman speaking.

"This is an executive position, "stated the sharply dressed Hispanic woman. "... And being *honored* with such a position you must act and dress the part. Clients must always, always," she vigorously emphasized "see you dressed in white! White represents purity and innocence and that is what our clients pay for.

There was that word, *"innocence"* again, Eloisa noted. They tossed it around like it was some bi product instead of an innate spiritual quality. As the lecture continued, she realized that they were draining children like batteries in order to charge someone else's needs! She felt sick inside and knew she had to make right, all of the tremendous wrongs she'd helped to perpetuate!

"They also want to feel in control," continued the woman.

"… Like the eternal teacher, always needed, appreciated and accepted. That is why we must be careful who we take into our homes for training. Continued violations of the persona of innocence could easily put us out of business and Mr. Harvey could never allow that. We are akin to the rare caviar business. People with rare appetites depend on us."

Eloisa, who had never taken a seat spoke up. "So, we feed them children instead?" The woman looked past her to the driver who handed over paper work. "It says here that you are Ms. Eloisa Castillo, property of Judge Erwin Mason. Is that true?"

"My name is Eloisa Mason and the Lord, Jesus Christ, owns me! So, now we are training kids to be raped, properly?!"

"Sit down, punta! Your son could be next!

"His father, Judge Mason, will protect him!"

Judge Mason answers to Thomas Harvey! And by the way, you don't even know where you are! So sit down and shut up!

The driver took her by the arm in a manner that suggested he was very serious, and led her to a lopsided rocking chair that sat atop rotting floorboards. This old splintered chair would serve as her weekly, summer perch to learn the do-s and don't-s of being a Madame in the child, sex trade industry.

Epiphany

Jentezen called the pilot and told him to fuel the plain. He knew from Erica's description that the classes on *"How To Become Madam Hoku"* were held at the old fishing cabin, deep in the hills of Tennessee.

When the plane arrived, the sun was rising in the magnificent Smokey Mountains, revealing golden, pink, and emerald hues. A limo was already present to carry them to the old fishing cabin, deep within the woods. Unfortunately, what was supposed to be a fifteen minute ride in comfort, turned into a vigorous walk through trees, over huge rocks and across a short suspension bridge. Jentezen didn't know the old roads were now blocked by bulging tree roots and mud slides.

They all seemed glad and then weighted by disappointment when their trek came to a sudden halt.

Curtis looked at Jentezen who stared at a burned out, wooden hull...

"Damn it!"

"Hold it." Came Billy's calm reassurance. He had made his way around the structure and into the charred interior. "They're onto us. This is a fresh fire. The sections where they used a concentration of accelerant is the most damaged. Whoever did this is an amateur, and was in a hurry."

Billy began to walk carefully across the length of the cabin, feeling the ash covered floorboards, buckle beneath his weight. Once again, he walked across, stopping near the center of the room because the Floorboards seemed weaker than the others. He knelt down, able to see between the gaps in the panels and insert his hand, sideways. A few tugs caused the brittle board to break, exposing what lie beneath. Billy whistled long and loud, alerting the others to come over and take a look. One by one they grabbed handfuls of letters that had been rolled into tubes and covered in a heavy duty, plastic wrap.

Curt's hands shook uncontrollably as he removed the now moist and dirty plastic and began reading...

"My name is Eloisa Castillo, from Texas. I am being forced to train children to be used by pedophiles. I was a victim myself and my own son, Cutis Castillo's safety is at risk! "

Jentezen's letter held a list of the students identities and the woman's name who brought them into *"Hoku* status." He was stunned that some of these people actually held national telethons and fundraisers to support children until they found homes. No one had asked any questions in all these years! But perhaps it was Billy's letter that would allow them to go home. He held a list of locations for all the assigned houses where the children were being kept.

"If we alert the authorities, my father will be notified within moments. He already knows the whereabouts of my plane."

"That's ok" Curt said. "If we can't try him in the court, we'll fry him in the media!" Curt began taking pictures of the letters and sending them to Phyllis Gordon, along with instructions for a *"Breaking News"* show in sex-trafficking case "Make sure you have a pow wow with Deborah about her human touch... Ok... Talk later..."

The next call chilled his bones. It was Thomas Harvey. "If you continue with this witch hunt, I will crucify

you and that filthy cunt you and my son seem to find so fascinating."

"Well, you dirty old bastard, may the best man win!"

Showtime

There was no sign of Deborah, anywhere! Both, she and Clive's cell phones went straight to voicemail. This meant Phyllis would have to fly solo with her guest who was an elderly, astute woman, that bore a striking resemblance to Robin Williams portrayal of the character, Mrs. Doubtfire

"5,4,3,2, and you are live," said the floor manager!

"Good morning, and thanks for joining Grace Magazine Live! Our guest this morning is Ms. Vermella Right, administrator for Tennessee's, *Perfect Angels Children's Home*. Thank you so much for joining us today, Ms. Right."

"My pleasure! When I got the call to talk about our facility, I couldn't resist!"

"I know that you have been the administrator of Perfect Angels since it opened in 1965. "

"That's right. We have plenty of experience," shaking her finger at the camera and smiling.

"I'm curious, Mrs. Right; where does an agency, such as yours get funding to stay in business for so long?"

"The normal places, I guess... Donations from generous philanthropist, our yearly telethon, fundraisers...."

That is so fortunate for the children. It was just this morning that documents were uncovered alleging that billionaire, Thomas Harvey is a major contributor to not only your facility, but many, many others as well!"

The large woman maintained her smile and calm demeanor. "Dear, our donors list is private, so I am not at liberty to share such information."

The floor manager was signaling Phyllis that phone lines were now open.

"Ok, we have a caller live. Go ahead, Nina..."

"My name is Nina Chambers and I was taken from my home in Grand Rapids Michigan, when I was four years old and placed in the Perfect Angels Children's Home.. Ms. Vermella Right told me my mother was dead and that she would take care of me."

"Is this true, Ms. Right?
"

"Yes," she answered with an unyielding confidence. "I remember Nina. Cute little, nervous thing; always making up stories."

"Well," said Nina, "you are going to love this story! They dressed all the children in white, all the time! We were not allowed to get dirty or eat things that kids eat! Instead, we learned perfect etiquette, how to apply makeup and what an adults private parts looked like. She trained us to be little prostitutes..."

Ms. Right couldn't sit quietly anymore! "How dare you bring me here to slander my good name! This child was placed in a good home, with good parents, who happened to be wealthy!"

"Yes," Nina continued. " The man you sent me to was very wealthy. There were many children in his home, from all over the world. I made friends with a boy named, Fong. When the man found out he made us have sex and told us we were his special dolls, and then, he would have sex with us... One of the other girls would hide in a closet and say The Lord's Prayer. Me and Fong would join her, saying it over and over until we felt the peace of God. Then, it was like he couldn't even touch us anymore. Or maybe it was that his touches couldn't affect us like they used to. At seventeen, Fong and I ran away, changed our name, and went to work for a foreign missionary group. Part of our mission is to secure the safety of children from pedophiles!

"You're just one of those religious freaks trying to push your cause," screamed the barrel of a woman!"

"Nina, what was the man's name who adopted you?

"Thomas Harvey"

The floor manager was signaling for commercial break, Ms. Vermella Right was running for the door and the producer was in a frenzy because the station was being flooded with calls from men and women with similar stories! They had, indeed, crucified Thomas Harvey in the media, and just as the bell of victory began to ring several FBI agents approached Phyllis and demanded that she come with them.

HE KIDNAPPED WHO?

Curt, Jentezen, and Billy were extremely concerned when the show returned from commercial break and highlights from previous shows were being broadcast.

"Someone tell me what the hell is going on," Curt screamed into his cell phone!

Bernadine was rattled by all the activity, especially by the FBI! "Where the hell are you, Curt Cavanaugh? The Feds are everywhere!"

"Darlin, I'm about forty thousand feet in the air, and about thirty minutes from Ohare. You're gonna have to hold it down."

Curt closed his eyes as a shield against the spew of profanity, almost glad that another call was coming in. "Bernie, hold on. I have to take this. Hello," he said to the other caller."

"Curtis, its Deborah…"

"Honey, I know who the hell you are. Why are you calling me *Curtis?*" And then, it hit him Deborah was in trouble. "Deborah, honey, where are you?"

"Mr. Harvey has taken the trouble to see that Clive and I were personally escorted to his compound. He said that you would be joining us shortly, and strongly suggested that I see what the holdup was."

Curt quickly muted the phone and looked at Jentezen. "Your Daddy has Deborah!" He unmuted and continued as calmly as possible. "Where are you, darlin?"

"He flew us into his compound, off the Newport Coast."

"Sit tight! I'm comin'!"

He clicked back over to Bernie. "Darlin', I'm gonna be a little bit longer than I thought…"

PELICAN BEACH MONSTERS WITH GOLF CLUBS AND MONSTERS IN SUITS

Jentezen's plane landed on the ocean side, strip without incident. Linen clad houseboys were already in position to help them deplane and give transport to the house.

Jentezen reacted in a very casual manner, as though it were just another afternoon. On the contrary, Billy's eyes never stopped scanning their surroundings. For this, Curt was grateful, because if they could get through this alive, it would be because of Billy.

Upon entering the premises, Billy hollered out, "Where you at, Preacher Boy?"

A butler then appeared, showing them into a sitting room. "If you will wait here, I'll get Mr. Harvey. "

This invitation didn't sit well with Billy who began a door to door search of the main floor.

Thomas Harvey strolled in through the French patio doors in the sitting room.

With a welcoming smile., he said "I'd like to thank you all for coming. I'm hoping we can put this nasty business to rest."

"This *nasty business*" is your occupation," Yelled Curt! "But right now, I don't give a damn about anything but Deborah! Where is she?"

"You seemed, only this morning to "give a damn" about my business, and all that I hold dear."

*

Billy was now on the second level swinging the doors open on a master suite. What he saw was a young girl, clad in sheer white chiffon and pearls sittting in the center of a huge poster bed. The red lipstick and rouge only accentuated her prepubescence, and gave Billy horrific pause as he pondered the weight of this situation.

"Baby girl, my name is Billy and I'm not going to hurt you."

Her head tilted to one side, causing a pile of dark curls to spill onto her shoulders. Then she smiled as Billy approached the bed. "My name is Lilly Harvey." This is my new home and Thomas Harvey is my new daddy."

Billy turned his face quickly, so she wouldn't see him swipe away the tear. "Lilly, I need your help. There was a very pretty lady, named Deborah, and a man named Clive that came here today. Do you know where they are?"

"Yes, Daddy Harvey said they were sleeping and we can't wake them."

Billy's face became a fixture of determination and ever present danger.

"Lilly, I want you to show Billy where Daddy Harvey is keeping those two people. I promise I won't tell," pretending to zip his lips...

"Shhhhh," Lilly whispered as she took his hand and led him to an adjoining room, "here they are."

Billy tried not to show signs of panic when he saw Deborah and Clive lying motionless on the floor. "Lilly, be a good girl and go back into the bedroom, he said gently."

 After she scurried away, Billy pulled out his gun, cocked it and backed into the room. He then knelt down to rouse Clive who remained eerily still. "Come on Preacher Boy! The Calvary is here!" "Mr. Westinghouse, you are just as rude as your grandfather. So, I can see how good manners would elude you in someone else's home."

Somewhere along the way, Old Man Harvey had found his way upstairs and into the master suite. Lilly was up in his liver stained arms with her face pressed into his neck.

"My granddaddy should of blown your ass to hell, fifty years ago! Now, what have you done to them?"

"They are in a chemically induced sleep. We've been administering this drug for years... Unfortunately, your friends shall remain this way until Mr. Castillo admits these shows of his are just publicity stunts to boost ratings. Now, please, join us back downstairs."

"You, old man, are getting desperate and sloppy."

" If you're not careful sonny, you could end up in that heap. I've got hidden cameras everywhere," turning Lilly around to reveal a camera compartment within her pearls. Security has been watching you ever since you walked in this house. Please put the gun down."

"With all-due respect, I will blow you and Lilly through the wall! Her life is fucked up anyway. So call them out here, with the shit to wake them up!"

Two large men, dressed in black entered the room and stood behind Thomas Harvey. One removed a syringe from his pocket and promptly injected Thomas Harvey in the neck, while the other took Lilly from his faltering grasp. The monster was then placed in bed, totally incapacitated.

"You may lower your weapon now, Mr. Westinghouse," came Jentezen's somber voice. "Mr. Harvey has fallen irreversibly Ill, after considering the full consequences of his crimes. It is now my responsibility to validate my father's crimes and condition for the proper authorities. In my father's absence I will have an influential seat on the board of directors that will make all of these issues, fade away.

Billy lowered his gun.

"Your friends are back on board the plane and my staff will see to Deborah and her assistants full recovery. As a matter of fact, you all we're never here.

Billy nodded his head, knowing that it was over, and also knowing that, if necessary, Jentezen could make him " go away" as well. "We will look after Deborah."

Jentezen nodded and said, "So will I."

FINDING OUR WAY HOME

The sensory perception of this dream included the smell of maple flavored, bacon frying in a pan, and the weight of her missing locket, hanging its comfort from her neck. There was a sweet peace in this dream, from which she never wanted to awake. But somewhere near, people were laughing with such joy that she wanted to join them! .

Rising from the cozy covers of her childhood, she managed slow steady steps to the stairwell that led down into Aunt Vicky's the kitchen.

Could it be that she was really home? In her woozy state, there, stood Clive alongside his father, Reverend Rodgers- laughing and hugging. Uncle Bob and Aunt Vickie sat at the table with Billy and Curt, and Mother Juna tended the frying bacon.

"Oh, my goodness," shouted Vickie! " Gurl, we thought you were gonna sleep through another day. . You been in and out of consciousness for almost two days! I don't know what big wigs you rubbin' elbows with, but a Senator Taylor from Texas sent a doctor to look in on you. He said he was so grateful for you all's help on a recent project that he would take care of all your medical bills! "

"Yeah," said her Uncle Bob. "Your friends here, said you had a terrible reaction to a vaccine. Said you passed out at work."

Curt stood and shook his head in the affirmative. "You gave us quite a scare. But you're fine now."

It was all coming back to her. She'd been drugged and her friends brought her home to recover. She gave a crooked smile and said, "Of course..."

"Don't just stand there," said Sister Juna.. "Come get some of these grits and some bacon! You lookin' real skinny! Guess TV stars don't eat!

"And it is Sunday mornin'," boomed Reverend Rodgers pulpit voice. "We have church this morning, Ms. Melody Baxter! So don't take all day."

Melody stood in the middle of the floor, not able to move, or speak, just shed tears of joy. Curt reached for her hand and pulled her close to him. "I should have known that you came from somewhere special.

Mother Juna sat Melody's plate on the table and planted a greasy, orange kiss on Curt's cheek. "Welcome to the family, young man!

Jentezen stood at the window of his Chicago penthouse gazing past the view of the marvelous skyline. Dora Floors stood behind him.

"Is there anything else sir?"

"I want weekly updates on Deborah and her friends."

"And that other matter?"

"He's in FBI custody and can't be roused. Keep him alive -for now"

The sequel to this novel, **HOW TO KILL A LIE** *is available now! See details about these books and other works by M. Handy @ COOTW.com*

Made in the USA
Lexington, KY
26 May 2017